Torch

Karen felt spittle hit her face as he climbed on, pinning her arms to the floor. The one behind her pulled up her jumper and stuffed it in her mouth. She wasn't going to scream anyway. If Emperor was dead she didn't care what they did to her.

When she came to, the room was thick with smoke.

She dragged herself onto her knees and crawled towards the door, hauling herself up by the handle, praying it wasn't locked. When she pulled it open, a long cold surge of oxygen smacked her face.

As the air rushed past, there was a high whistling sound like a train going through a tunnel. Seconds later the backdraft hit her, demolishing the hoarding and propelling her forward in a ball of flame.

About the author

Lin Anderson began writing whilst working as a teacher, and now writes full time. *Torch* is her second novel, and the second to feature forensic scientist Rhona Macleod.

Also by Lin Anderson:

Driftnet
Deadly Code

LIN ANDERSON

Torch

HODDER

Copyright © 2004 by Lin Anderson

First published in Great Britain in 2004 by Luath Press Ltd

First published in paperback in 2007 by Hodder & Stoughton
A division of Hodder Headline

The right of Lin Anderson to be identified as the Author
of the Work has been asserted by her in accordance with
the Copyright, Designs and Patents Act 1988.

A Hodder paperback

4

A CIP catalogue record for this title
is available from the British Library

ISBN 978 0340 92237 8

Typeset in Plantin by Hewer Text UK Ltd, Edinburgh
Printed and bound by Clays Ltd, St Ives plc

Hodder Headline's policy is to use papers that are natural, renewable
and recyclable products and made from wood grown in sustainable
forests. The logging and manufacturing processes are expected to
conform to the environmental regulations of the country of origin.

Hodder & Stoughton Ltd
A division of Hodder Headline
338 Euston Road
London NW1 3BH

Thanks to Emma R. Hart,
BSc, MSc, Forensic Science for her inside knowledge.

To Detective Inspector Bill Mitchell

I

IT WAS STARTING to rain. Emperor looked up reproachfully as an icy drop hit his muzzle.

'Okay, boy.'

Karen slipped the penny whistle into her pack and rolled up the blanket. She counted the money in the hat. Shit! Ten pence short.

The Alsatian was pacing, anxious to be away, anticipating a meal. She set off, head down, into the rain. There was an empty building near the west end of Princes Street. She had been sleeping behind the hoarding for the past couple of weeks.

The dog started to jump about as they got near Burger King; tongue hanging out, eyes bright with excitement.

The door opened and a guy came out, stumbling over Emperor, nearly dropping the precious cardboard box. He smiled when he saw her.

'Hey, Karen! You eating?'

It was the *Big Issue* seller from outside Waverley Station. He'd told her his name. Jaz. She liked that he was named after music. He'd asked her name and she'd told him. But that was all.

Karen shook her head.

'What about Emperor?'

'He's eaten.'

Emperor was sniffing the box, so she started to walk on.

'I'll see you later,' Jaz shouted after her. When she was far enough away, she hugged Emperor and he licked her face. 'I promise, Emps. Tomorrow. First thing. Ten pence more, and it's yours.'

The hoarding was plastered with posters advertising Edinburgh's New Year. She waited until no one was looking, then slipped in behind, swept the litter off the step and spread out the blanket. Emperor waited patiently while she settled herself, then lay down beside her.

Through a hole in the hoarding, an illuminated Edinburgh Castle looked down on her like a picture in a fairy tale.

When she opened her eyes Emperor was alert beside her, his ears pricked up, a low growl in his throat. Someone was moving about behind the door.

'Easy boy,' she whispered.

She waited, a hand on Emperor's head. A security guard would check the door then go away, and they could go back to sleep.

As the door opened, she quickly reached for her pack and blanket.

'Go, Emps.'

She was about to follow when she was grabbed from behind.

'Not so fucking fast!'

Emps had heard her scream and was coming back, but he was too late. The man yanked her inside and kicked the door shut in the dog's face.

'Look what I found.'

The other two men turned and stared at her. The smile on the blond one's face turned her stomach. The one in the leather jacket was excited about something, but it wasn't her. Behind them, Emperor was barking and scraping at the door.

Leather Jacket said: 'Get the dog!'

The blond one picked up a metal bar and opened the door, just enough to let Emps get his head in. The agonised yelp as the bar hit the dog's muzzle brought Karen to her knees.

Now he was finished with the dog, the blond guy was looking her up and down.

'Seems a shame to waste her.'

Leather Jacket was walking away, his mind on something else. 'Make it fast,' he shouted.

The one holding her laughed. 'Only way he knows.'

'Shut the fuck up!'

Karen felt spittle hit her face as he climbed on, pinning her arms to the floor. The one behind pulled up her jumper and stuffed it in her mouth. She wasn't going to scream anyway. If Emperor was dead she didn't care what they did to her.

When she came to, the room was thick with smoke.

She dragged herself onto her knees and crawled towards the door, hauling herself up by the handle, praying it wasn't locked. When she pulled it open, a long cold surge of oxygen smacked her face.

As the air rushed past, there was a high whistling sound like a train going through a tunnel. Seconds later the backdraft hit her, demolishing the hoarding and propelling her forward in a ball of flame.

2

DR RHONA MACLEOD switched on the data projector, inserted the crime scene tape in the video recorder and pressed 'Play'.

The output on the large wall-screen was as good as if she had been at the cinema. Police photographers routinely recorded a body's position and injuries, sometimes catching those who moved quietly in the background – the scene of crime officers, the pathologist, the forensic expert like herself.

The body on the screen was that of a young male. He lay in the pugilistic attitude typical of fire victims; the arms extended from the shoulders, the forearms partially flexed in a boxer's stance. In close up, his skin had odd white patches left unburnt, although intense heat had ruptured his skull and split his ankle joint, so that the right foot was free of his leg.

She had examined fluid from his blistered skin but the results were puzzling. Some behaved as if they had been made after death, with little fluid to extract and no positive protein reaction on test-tube heating. Others behaved as though they had been created while he was still alive.

It was common for murderers to believe they could

cover a death with fire, but fire did not consume everything. Even the slightest traces of accelerant could be sampled and identified. The difficulty lay in deciding whether a chemical detected at the scene was there normally, or for the purpose of starting the fire.

Rhona stopped the tape and switched it for the home video Detective Inspector Bill Wilson had sent round. While the hullabaloo was going on round the burning Glasgow tenement, someone in the crowd had had the sense or the morbid curiosity to capture it on video.

She might have been watching a television drama, except that the expressions of fear and determination on the faces of the firemen were real and the flames that roared from the roof of this building were not computer-enhanced.

The owner of the camcorder had zoomed in on a couple on the second floor. The man was holding a baby out of the window in a desperate attempt to help it breathe. The look of terror on the woman's face distressed Rhona, even though she knew all three members of the household had escaped unharmed.

Rhona concentrated on the flames, their colour, shape, direction and intensity. The characteristics of a fire could provide clues to its origin. She played the tape through once more, pausing periodically, taking notes, knowing someone in the fire department would be doing exactly the same thing.

Chrissy McInsh, her scientific officer, stuck her red head round the door at seven.

'I'm starving. Fancy something to eat?

'We could try the new Chinese takeaway on Gibson Street?'

'What do you fancy?'

Rhona shrugged. 'You decide.'

While Chrissy went to order, she began to clear away the debris of the day. She checked her email once more in case there was a message from Chemistry about the tests on the fire debris, knowing it was too soon. This was the time in an investigation when patience was most needed. And when she had it least. Outside, midwinter darkness enveloped the Kelvingrove Museum and Art Gallery and the neighbouring park. The park was frequented by families during the day, but it became the location for a different type of pleasure after dark. Tonight the ill-lit paths were deserted.

There was one message in her inbox. No subject title, and she didn't recognise the address. She contemplated dumping it. In an attempt to cut down on the spread of viruses IT services had advised the deletion of any unofficial looking mail, but curiosity got the better of her. It was a string of capital letters. I C H B U N R T E B T H.

She'd had two like this already and deleted them both. She tried for a couple of minutes to make the characters into a word, then gave up and saved it. If another one arrived, she would try and puzzle it out.

'It's got to involve drugs,' Rhona said.

Chrissy looked up from her lemon chicken.

'Because in that part of Glasgow it usually does?'

Rhona nodded. 'If I'm right and the blistering on the victim's wrists was nothing to do with the fire, what does that suggest to you?'

Chrissy shook her head. 'No idea.'

'Drug barons like to control their patch. Beatings and torture are ways of doing that.'

'Dr Sissons said the death looked like a heart attack.'

'Or a heroin overdose.'

Chrissy pushed her food away.

'Can we leave the post-mortem for tonight? My stomach feels funny.'

'I think it's the chicken.' Rhona made a face and gestured towards the bin.

The flat was in darkness when Rhona got home. Sean would have already left for his gig at the Ultimate Jazz Club. The ansaphone was flashing in the hall and there was a note beside it. There was fresh pasta in the fridge if she was hungry. He'd see her at the club.

She pressed the button to save the messages and went through to the kitchen, wishing she hadn't succumbed to the Chinese takeaway.

A full bottle of red wine was uncorked and waiting for her. Sean never drank before a gig. Playing the saxophone was his high. That, sex and cooking in equal proportions, and sometimes at the same time.

She opened the bedroom window a little and pulled the curtains, got undressed and climbed into bed.

Rhona felt the cat before she heard it; a long soft tail brushing her face, then the press of paws as it settled on her chest. She opened her mouth to protest and a hand slid over it, smothering her complaint. The cat jumped with an angry miaow to the floor.

'Ssh, now. You can't blame the cat for lying where it did.'

'Sean!'

'Who else would it be?'

'What time is it?'

'Nearly three.' He touched her lips.

'You're frozen,' she protested.

'You can warm me up.'

He quickly pulled off his clothes. She caught a glimpse of chest, of thigh. The duvet flicked back, there was a rush of cool air and then Sean pressed his naked body against hers. She shivered with pleasure and cold.

'You shouldn't go to bed and leave the window open,' he whispered into her hair. 'It's not safe.'

'We look down on a convent. God will protect us.'

He laughed. 'Who's the Irish Catholic here?' and buried his face in her neck.

His chilled lips travelled downwards to draw in her nipple and suck it. A ripple of anticipation encircled her hips. She felt him stir against her and traced his thigh with her fingers.

He flipped her, pinning her below him.

'I want to play a tune.'

She smiled. 'What's wrong with your saxophone?'

'Your notes are sweeter.'

Rhona rolled over and flicked on the light.

'I was going to tell you,' Sean said evenly.

'When? After we had sex?' she asked accusingly.

'I only got confirmation this morning.' He was placating her, as usual. 'You said you were coming to the club. I would have told you then.'

Rhona was silent.

'It's a good gig, Rhona. I'll only be away a few days.'

'I know. It's just . . .'

'What?'

He waited, sensing something else was wrong.

'I've arranged to meet Liam,' she said quietly.

The name of her son hung between them.

'He's coming north to visit a school friend before he leaves for his gap year in Africa.' She paused. 'He wants to meet me.'

Sean was struggling to understand her distress.

'But you've wanted this for so long,' he said, puzzled.

'And now it's happened . . .' her voice tailed off. She couldn't articulate her fear, even to Sean. What if Liam didn't like her? What if he hated her for what she'd done?

'Your son will love you.'

She wondered if he believed that or was saying it to avoid any further discussion.

'Love the mother who gave him away?'

He pulled her to him, pressing her head to his chest. His heart beat gently in her ear.

'It'll be okay,' he murmured.

Sean's answer to everything.

'And if it's not?' she insisted.

There was no reply as Sean drifted into post-coital sleep, his mind already in Amsterdam.

A knot had formed in her chest. She shouldn't have mentioned meeting Liam. What if it all went wrong?

She waited until she heard the soft measured sound of sleep, then extracted herself carefully from beneath Sean's arm and got up.

Rain splattered the window so that the lights of Glasgow ran into one another like a watery kaleido-scope. Her naked shadow stood alone, reflected in the glass. She mouthed the words, *we are born alone and we die alone*, even as something inside her wished Sean had said, 'You'll always have me.'

3

WHEN DI BILL Wilson contacted her early the next morning, they had to transfer the call to the Chemistry Lab where she'd been with Dr Spenser since first thing.

Spenser was definite. It was a Class A fire.

'So, mainly paper, wood and fabric?' Rhona suggested.

The forensic chemist nodded. Rhona wondered if the long granite face would ever be split by a smile. 'And no evidence of hydrocarbons?' He shook his head. 'Only the normal traces from household goods.' 'In the video,' Rhona paused, already knowing he would put her down, 'I thought the smoke looked black.'

He gave her a sideways look. 'You've been studying too many American flame charts.'

'So how do you think the fire started?'

'You'll have to discuss that with the fire investigator. As far as I'm concerned there is nothing chemical to suggest that this was a wilful fire incident.' Rhona tried another tack. 'We found evidence of alcohol in the remains of the victim's jacket, especially round the wrists.'

'Maybe he couldn't hold his drink.'

Rhona didn't laugh. Spenser never made jokes intentionally.

'Drugs?'

'We're still running tests, but there's nothing to suggest there were any on the premises.'

When Spenser's equally dour assistant called her to the phone she found Bill's friendly voice a pleasant relief.

'How's cheerful Charlie?' Bill asked.

Rhona kept her voice neutral, for the sake of inter-lab relations. 'Same as usual.'

'And the tests on the fire debris?'

'No evidence to suggest an accelerant was used,' she told him.

'The pathology report says the victim died of an overdose.'

'And the fire?'

'He dropped a cigarette, and whoosh?'

It didn't sound right to her. 'What about the blisters on his wrists?'

'Accidental.'

Bill was baiting her to see what she would come up with.

'You and I both know another accidental fire in three months in an area up for redevelopment is suspiciously convenient.'

'We have nothing to substantiate that at this stage.'

That would be just what his superior would say.

'So why did you phone?'

'I was coming to that.'

Rhona had worked with Bill on many cases since

she'd arrived in Glasgow after her stint in the DNA Laboratory in Birmingham. She had thrown herself into the new job, relishing the responsibility for drawing the different branches of forensics together. The relationship between the forensic department and the CID was good because of Bill.

'Dave Gallagher's had a heart attack,' he told her.

'My God. Is he okay?'

'He's out of danger, but he'll be off work for six weeks at least.' He paused. 'He's been working on the recent Edinburgh fires. There was another one last night.'

'I heard on the news this morning.'

She knew what he was going to ask.

'I'm pretty tied up here, Bill.'

'I know.' He sounded apologetic but resolved. 'But if there's even a remote chance there's a link between their fires and ours . . .'

He waited.

'Okay,' she conceded. Wilful fire-raising at the same time in Scotland's two major cities was unlikely to be coincidence.

'Great.' Bill's voice had grown cautious. 'Severino MacRae is the chief fire investigator. You'll be working with him.'

The best thing to come out of Edinburgh is the train to Glasgow, or so say the citizens of the dear green place. Of course, that can be reversed. Cities forty-six miles apart, one wholly respectable and the other totally irreverent, the dichotomy of the Scottish urban psyche.

Rhona turned from the train window and refused the offer of coffee from the trolley. The lemon chicken from the night before was taking its toll.

She had called Sean from the station to explain her sudden departure to Edinburgh.

'Will you be back before I leave for Amsterdam?'

'I don't think so.'

'I'll give you a call when I get there.'

'I'm staying at Greg's.'

'Okay. I'll see you in a week, then.'

The call had ended in awkward silence.

Rhona turned to the window as the train drew away from Linlithgow Station. Low December sunlight brushed the imposing walls of Linlithgow Palace and danced on the choppy waters of the nearby loch. One summer when she was eight or nine, her father had brought her here for the day. She'd stood in the big courtyard with its wonderful fountain and tried to imagine what it was like to be the princess destined to be Queen of Scots.

She wondered, not for the first time, what her beloved adoptive parents would think of her now, had they been alive. They had never known about Liam. She'd kept her pregnancy a secret because Edward, her lover at the time, wasn't ready to be a father. She had to finish her degree and establish her career. Their relationship had been washed away in the misery and guilt she'd felt after giving up her baby for adoption. Like her, Liam had had adoptive parents who loved him. For her, it had been enough. But for Liam?

Edinburgh Waverley was busy with tourists in town for *The Biggest Hogmanay Party in the World*. A young guy was selling the *Big Issue* on the Waverley steps. Rhona thrust a two pound coin into his hand. He tried to give her change, but she waved it away and he smiled his thanks.

The east end of Princes Street was almost devoid of traffic. A little way along she realised why. The police had cordoned off a section of road and were directing traffic onto George Street.

When Rhona reached the cordon she showed the constable on duty her ID then headed for the incident tent.

4

SEVERINO MACRAE REACHED for the phone on the third ring, an Americanism he'd picked up at some stupid management course they'd insisted he go on. Never before the third ring, never after. The habit had stuck.

'Of course I'm up,' Sev threw back the covers. 'Already been for a jog.' He lifted the open whisky bottle from the bedside cabinet with his left hand and threw some into a nearby glass. 'It's better than sex, Sergeant. You should try it.' He moved the receiver out of the way. The alarm clock showed nine. 'I've an appointment at eleven thirty.' He held the phone in the crook of his neck while he poured another shot. 'Okay, I'll be there. Just tell them to touch nothing. Got that? Nothing. And Sergeant? Tell MacFarlane not to piss on the embers or I'll cut off his dick.'

The bottle was empty. He threw it in the bin on his way to the shower. There was always a chance Gillian might come round. He didn't want her to think he lived like a pig just because she had left him and taken their daughter Amy with her.

The water on his head woke him up enough to remember Gallagher was still in hospital recovering from his heart attack. Looking at Gallagher's colour last night, Sev guessed his colleague would be out of the game for at least six weeks. So no forensic, or at least no forensic with Gallagher's experience of fires. It was as if this particular fire-raiser knew he had a clear run.

Sev dried himself and looked for a clean shirt. The hangers in the wardrobe stared emptily back at him. Shit. He'd left the six new non-iron shirts from Marks and Spencer in his office. He picked last night's off the floor and sniffed it. If he kept his jacket on he might avoid knocking anyone out.

Before he left, he phoned Gillian. He knew before he started to speak it was a hopeless case. There was frost forming on the other end of the line.

'What makes you think I would cancel?' He tried to sound offended.

Silence.

'I might be a bit late, that's all.' Sev looked at the clock. 'Look, I'll be there. Right? Eleven thirty.'

He rang off and headed for the door. The postman had already delivered an ominous pile of mail. Sev kicked the half dozen brown envelopes out of the way and a small white one slipped into view. He picked it up, thinking the big round writing might be Amy's. Since his ejection from the family home, Amy had taken to sending him small notes with big illustrations. Mostly they consisted of tales of her hamster and its various methods of escape. Every time one arrived, Sev's guts twisted a little tighter.

The writing wasn't Amy's, and there was no postage stamp. Sev opened the door and looked out, trying to remember when he'd heard the letter-box rattle. When he was on the phone to Gillian? The stairwell stared back at him, silent and empty. Whoever delivered the letter was long gone.

Sev waited until he was in the car before he opened it, his mind already assimilating this latest development in the letter saga. So now the bastard knew where he lived? Sev examined the last few days. Where he had gone, when he had come home, the people he'd talked to. Had he been followed, watched, as he muddled his way through what had become his life since Gillian threw him out? He began to unfold the white paper, already knowing what it would say. The texture felt strange, as if something had been spilt on it. He held the paper to his nose and sniffed.

'Jesus!'

Thank God Gillian had thrown him out. If she hadn't, some crazy bastard would have been pushing semen-encrusted letters through her letter-box instead of his.

The usual message spewed across the stiffened paper. All the key words were there. Fire. Bitches. Sex. This one hated women so much he needed an inferno to get a hard-on. And that's exactly what he had done last night: lit one.

Sev parked his old Saab next to the mortuary van, wondering why the sergeant hadn't mentioned any bodies when he called him, just the extent of the fire and its prominent position on Princes Street. The building had been lying empty for months. Rumour had it development was being held up because the original façade had to be retained. An expensive investment for somebody.

Detective Inspector Peter MacFarlane came towards him as he climbed out of the Saab.

MacFarlane looked in need of a good night's sleep. The mortuary van might have been there for him. Sev stepped over the yellow incident ribbon and nodded in the direction of the police tent, constructed over the pavement that bordered the famous Princes Street Gardens.

'There was a body,' MacFarlane told them as they walked. 'A young girl. She must have been nearby when it blew.' MacFarlane looked sick.

The mental picture hadn't escaped Sev either.

He turned on the first retch, thinking MacFarlane was emptying his stomach, but MacFarlane wasn't the one being sick. To their left a gate led into the Gardens where a path cut through a bed of roses, a riot of colour for summer tourists but in December bare, pruned and colourless, except for the blonde head and blue jacket among the bushes.

'She took a look inside the tent while she was waiting for you.'

'Waiting for me?'

'That's right.' Sev could hear caution in MacFarlane's voice. 'Visiting forensic from Glasgow.'

Sev didn't like the sound of that, particularly not after the latest epistle from the arsonist.

'Send her home,' he said.

'What?'

'I said send her home.' Sev wasn't in the mood to go into details. 'I don't want a woman on this case.'

MacFarlane was getting shirty. 'You need a forensic. She's been working on the Glasgow fires. There may be a link . . .'

'I don't care. I don't want a woman,' Sev said.

'I thought sexism was only rife in the Police Force.'

'Leave it out, MacFarlane. I have my reasons.'

'Well now's your chance to tell them directly to Dr MacLeod.'

The woman coming towards him was exactly what Sev didn't want. Sexy, her intelligent eyes meeting his, examining him.

Rhona sat at a table while MacRae went to get some coffee. Even the furniture in the café smelt deep-fried. She concentrated on breathing as shallowly as possible. The toilets were right behind her. Close enough for an emergency.

When MacRae came back he was carrying a tray with two cups, a pot of coffee and the full works; bacon, sausage, black pudding, fried bread and a double portion of eggs. He laid the tray on the table and made a big show of splashing tomato sauce over everything.

'Sure you don't want some?'

Rhona shook her head. 'No thanks. I've eaten.'

'It didn't stay down long.' He forked a sausage. 'You going to do that when we get inside the building?' He wagged the burnt sausage in her face then plunged it in the tomato sauce.

Rhona ignored the jibe.

'So, how long have you been doing this job?'

'I've been in Glasgow three years . . .' She began the usual answer but he didn't give her a chance to finish.

'Three years. Wow. Long time.' She ignored the sarcasm. 'I was seven years at the Forensic Lab in Birmingham before that.'

He took another bite of the sausage. 'You married?'

She hadn't been expecting that one.

'Thought not,' he said when she didn't answer.

'What's that supposed to mean?'

'No time?' he suggested, the sarcasm back.

'No inclination,' she said firmly.

He laid down the knife and fork and reached for her hand, catching her completely off guard. The hand that held hers was warm and dry, the grasp firm but not tight. He pulled it towards the coffee pot and held it there for a moment.

'Ever been burned?'

She pulled free.

'Yes . . . no . . . not really.'

'What does that mean, not really?'

'It means, nothing serious.'

He shook his head. 'You don't know fire until you've been burned.'

'I disagree.'

'Gallagher had ten years' experience in this game.'

'And *he's* a man.'

'With a strong stomach.'

If she hadn't been so angry, Rhona would have laughed. 'I wasn't sick because of the body.'

'This isn't a job for a pregnant woman. There are fumes, asbestos dust . . .'

He was unbelievable. Rhona lifted her coat from the back of the chair.

'Where are you going?'

This time she had caught him off guard.

'I'm going to do what I came to do. My job.'

MacRae wasn't defeated yet.

'No assistant of mine goes into that building until it's structurally safe.'

Rhona was aware that at least half the café was listening to their argument. She raised her voice for the benefit of the other half.

'You'd better find your assistant and tell them that, then.'

'Look, lady . . .'

'No, you look, Mr MacRae. I am not your "lady" assistant. I am a forensic scientist. You, I believe, are a fire investigator. Together we can find out why and how this fire happened or I can catch the next train to Glasgow. Either way I'm happy, although I think your superiors may not be pleased if I choose the second option.'

MacRae's expression didn't change. He stood up and looked at his watch.

'I have an appointment to keep,' he said. 'No one goes into the building until I get back.'

Rhona watched him leave, irritated with herself for handling things badly. MacRae didn't want her there, that was obvious. Exactly why, she wasn't so sure.

*   *   *

Sev got to the Family Reconciliation Office at eleven thirty-five. It wasn't soon enough for Gillian. The meeting had started badly and was deteriorating every time he opened his mouth. The counsellor was doing her best, but what a sixty-year-old woman with hair like the Queen could tell him about marriage wasn't what he wanted to know. He wanted to see Gillian alone, not as part of a family reconciliation sandwich.

The counsellor wasn't giving up. Awkward customers like him were her bread and butter.

'Mr MacRae. I believe you would like to discuss your daughter.'

That was rich.

'No. I'd like to see my daughter.'

Gillian wasn't letting him away with that.

'You do see Amy. You see her more now than when you were at home.'

The way she said it sounded as if he had left home by choice. Sev stopped himself blurting that out, just as a fire engine went past, siren blaring. His impulse was to go to the window but he already knew which direction it was heading. Besides, Gillian would be watching his reaction, ready to jump on it like a dog on a bone. He sat still.

'You're not listening,' she said.

He tried to keep his tone patient. He sounded long-suffering. 'I am listening.'

'Not to us.'

It was the counsellor's turn.

'Mr MacRae, your wife is concerned about the effect your work has on your family.'

'I have to work,' he said. 'Everyone has to work.'

'Not twenty-four hours a day.'

Gillian was right but it didn't make it any easier.

Sev was waiting for the other fire engine, knowing it was only a matter of time. Tollcross was a good unit. Fast. The second engine would be right behind the first. It was.

'Like now,' Gillian said, vindicated.

Sev tried to smile, feeling his face shift under the weight of it. Gillian was right. He was working just now. He was working out what the addition of a female forensic would do to the fire-raiser's view of the current situation. If the fire-raiser liked watching him, he would like watching the woman even more.

MacRae dragged himself back to the present. 'I'm not working right now,' he lied.

'No, but you're thinking about work right now.'

The counsellor came back in like a diligent referee.

'It would seem important to both of you that the issue of your daughter is resolved,' she suggested.

'That's why we should discuss custody.' Sev watched fear blossom in Gillian's eyes as he said this, and was sorry. But he wasn't going to back down on this one. Gillian might be giving up on him but he couldn't live without his daughter.

'It's not called custody now, Mr MacRae. It's called residence and . . .'

Sev wasn't interested in what it was called.

'If she wants to break up the marriage, then I want to look after Amy.'

'That wouldn't work.'

He willed Gillian to see how he really felt behind the anger and the bravado and the hurt. 'I don't want to be a part-time father,' he said, and meant it.

But Gillian was there before he finished the sentence.

'You always were.'

The drill of his mobile saved the counsellor the bother of another intervention. It was MacFarlane. Sev had left him in charge of the scene and Dr MacLeod until he got back. He suspected MacFarlane had his work cut out.

'Just keep her away from the building until I get there.'

When he turned back, Gillian was on her feet.

'I take it you're leaving?' she asked.

'I can wait till we're finished.'

'We're finished now.'

'I suggest,' the counsellor was brisk, 'we start ten minutes earlier next time. Make up the time lost today.'

Sev followed Gillian down the steps. He could tell how bad she felt by the stiffness of her back. He wanted to put his arm around her, hold her. Instead, he stood beside her on the pavement with his hands in his pockets.

'I'll see you Friday then.'

Gillian nodded and turned to go.

'If you want to see Amy before then . . .' she looked back at him, 'she's been asking for you.'

'I'll phone and arrange something for tonight,' he promised.

'Just because we're in a mess, doesn't mean Amy has to be,' Gillian said quietly.

Her vulnerability made MacRae take her hand. She didn't pull it away.

'Gillian . . .' he began.

His mobile vibrated against his chest. He swore. It would be MacFarlane again.

Gillian's voice was resigned. 'You'd better answer it.'

'I don't have to.' He sounded desperately torn, even to himself.

Gillian gave him a look that suggested that in the end he didn't have any real choice.

'Okay,' he reached in his jacket. 'Give me a minute.'

She nodded, but when he turned back after speaking to MacFarlane she had gone.

5

JAZ WALKED THROUGH the railway station, shouting a 'Hi' to the woman on the WH Smith counter. He bought a coffee at the kiosk on the corner and sat down on a bench to drink it. He was later than usual this morning and the rush was over. Rush hour wasn't good for him anyway. The punters were in too much of a hurry to get to work. He just got in the way.

Now was the time for shoppers and tourists. Most of the shoppers were regular as clockwork. He even knew some of their names. Mrs Paterson from Musselburgh, off the train every Monday at eleven o'clock. She always bought a *Big Issue* from him. Sometimes she gave him a home-baked scone or cake. Even complained to him about her husband. Jaz didn't mind. At least Mrs Paterson spoke to him like he was a human being.

He finished his coffee and made for the exit, just as the 10.20 from Glasgow pulled in. He wanted to be ready with the magazines. Glaswegians had a reputation for generosity.

From his pitch he could see the Edinburgh skyline. The castle and law courts to the left, the central sweep of the gardens leading to the art gallery, and on the right the Scott Monument. Tourists loved this view. Jaz would watch them emerge from the bowels of the station into daylight and the sudden splendour of the city. The Athens of the north, he'd read that somewhere. In summer it was occasionally true.

Today was dull, with a cold wind from the east and the odd spit of rain. The tourists didn't care. As soon as they spotted the castle, the cameras were out. If only he had ten pence for every photo taken of Edinburgh Castle, Jaz thought.

It was then he noticed the smoke. A blanket of it lay to the north-west of the city. He was so busy staring at it, he didn't notice the pretty blonde woman trying to buy a magazine. She handed him a two pound coin and he tried to give her change but she wouldn't take it.

He stayed on his pitch until curiosity got the better of him. At least half a dozen of his regulars had already asked if he'd heard about the fire on Princes Street. The police had cordoned off part of the road but you could get a view from the Gardens, they said.

It seemed he wasn't the only one keen to get a look. Around the Ross Bandstand half of Edinburgh seemed to be spending lunchtime in the Gardens, despite the cold weather.

Jaz wasn't surprised to see Emperor standing by the railing at the top of the steep bank of roses. He'd half-expected to see Karen in the Gardens anyway. She usually brought Emps in for a run during the day. But not as early as this. Lunchtime was busy for her. People strolling along Rose Street liked to hear her play.

The dog started to howl, a mournful sound. Jaz hurried up the steep bank. A tent was erected on the pavement, and just left of it the dog was tied to a railing.

Jaz stuck his hand through and rubbed the dog's ears. 'Hey, Emps.'

'Watch out, son. He might bite.' A policeman had emerged from the tent and was coming towards him.

'No he won't. Will you, boy?'

The dog stopped whining and started to growl as the policeman approached.

'Where's Karen?' Jaz was talking to the dog but it was the policeman who answered.

'Who's Karen?'

Jaz stood up. 'Emps belongs to a girl called Karen.'

The policeman was interested. 'Is this Karen a friend of yours?'

'I know her.'

'Could you come round here and tell us a bit more about Karen?'

'Why? What's happened?' Jaz was suddenly frightened. Karen wouldn't tie Emps to a railing and abandon him. There was a funny look on the policeman's face. 'A girl . . . we think she was asleep in the doorway when the fire . . .'

'Karen's dead?' Jaz felt dazed. A picture of Karen formed in his mind, her fingers coaxing music from the whistle, her eyes closed, her mind somewhere else. Always somewhere away from here and now.

'We need to contact her family to identify . . .'

Jaz's brain was stupid with pain. 'Karen hasn't got a family.'

'Everybody's got a family, son.'

'That's shite!' The shout caught in his throat. 'Karen had no one,' he looked down, 'except Emperor.' The dog whined and pawed at his leg.

'What's going to happen to Emperor?'

'We've called the RSPCA.'

'They'll put him down.'

The policeman was getting out his notebook. 'Look son. You give me your name and address. If we can't find a relative, maybe you could identify the girl.'

Jaz spoke quietly, his mind already made up. 'Give me the dog.'

'I can't do that . . .'

Jaz was on his knees, his hands through the railings, wrestling with the rope attached to Emperor's collar. The dog was jumping about, pulling at the rope. Another policeman was on his way over. The one beside him was trying persuasion tactics.

'Look, son. Come over and give us a contact address. I'll tell the RSPCA that you're interested in the dog and . . .'

The rope was almost free.

'Come on, Emps. Come on, boy.'

Jaz started to run.

Behind him the dog, suddenly frantic, tore at the remains of the knot. Jaz heard the policeman shout as Emps cleared the spikes and landed in the rose bushes. Jaz kept on running.

6

RHONA HAD BEEN hanging around now for almost an hour. DI MacFarlane had been pleasant but firm. No one was permitted to enter the building until they were sure it wasn't in imminent danger of collapse.

They weren't waiting for an inspection team to give the all-clear. Rhona was sure of that. They were waiting for MacRae to return from wherever he had disappeared to an hour before. She'd spotted MacFarlane on the phone, decidedly rattled. No doubt checking in with his lord and master, she thought unkindly.

After walking round the building a couple of times, she retired to a police car with a cup of coffee from a doughnut vendor. Through the windscreen, she watched scene of crime officers sifting through the piles of sodden debris that littered the pavement, an unpleasant but necessary business. At least MacRae had let them make a start on that. She'd already introduced herself to the two men involved. They'd worked with Gallagher and seemed to know what they were doing.

Her meeting with the pathologist had been less satisfactory. Brisk and professional, he gave nothing away. She'd eventually mentioned her work with Dr

Sissons. At the name of his Glasgow counterpart, the doctor raised an eyebrow.

The voice was old school Edinburgh. Chances were he had never been to Glasgow in his life.

'You've come through from the west to help us.'

It made her sound like the cavalry.

'There may be a link between the two spates of fire-raising.'

'I take it your main concern is the fire and not the death of the girl.' 'Well,' she hesitated, knowing what she was about to ask was not strictly protocol. 'The two are related.' He waited while she chose her words. 'I was hoping I might sit in on the post-mortem.' 'Is that absolutely necessary?' The man looked as though he had just discovered a bad smell.

'It might help.'

He stared at her, then nodded.

'I have two to do today. It won't be until tomorrow morning. 7.30.'

Chrissy wasn't telling her anything she didn't know already. Rhona moved the mobile to her other ear and reached for the coffee cup she'd stuck in the door pocket.

'Okay, Chrissy, but you haven't met the man. I'm going to insist all samples come through to you. That way I won't have Valentino breathing down my neck. And no, I do *not* think he's sexy. If you saw him dipping a charred sausage in a blob of tomato sauce you wouldn't think so either.'

The noises on the other end of the phone suggested

Chrissy did not believe her. Denials always made matters worse with Chrissy.

'I'll have to go. My caveman's back. And Chrissy. Don't buy any more of those takeaways. I spent half the morning being sick.'

Rhona dropped the window on MacRae's second knock.

The voice was irritated. 'You ready?'

'Of course.'

'Let's go then.'

Rhona wondered if the anger radiating from his body was specifically directed at her.

He turned back as she shut the door of the police car.

'I suggest you bring a plastic bag. No one is allowed to pee, spit, shit, cough or vomit once inside the building.'

Rafters gaped above Rhona like the broken ribs of a huge whale. Underfoot, the floor was a spongy mass of sodden debris.

MacRae led the way, followed by MacFarlane who joined them at the door. The acrid smell caught at Rhona's throat. Despite being familiar with fire scenes, the devastation fire wrought always surprised her. At a normal murder scene it was the victim that lay mutilated. Here, the building was the victim.

Along the wall of what must have been a reception area, a set of metal shelves were twisted by the strength of the fire. A filing cabinet stood open, buckled by the heat.

MacFarlane spoke first.

'One of the firemen said the colour of the flames was wrong.'

'Whatever was burning wasn't what should have been in here?' Rhona asked.

MacFarlane nodded.

'The building was being renovated and the owner was taking a long time about it. The preservation people were being awkward.'

'You think it might be an insurance job?'

They both looked at MacRae for confirmation.

'I don't think anything. But I sure as hell smell something.'

MacFarlane had picked his way across the debris to the remains of a doorway on the left.

'Take a look at this, Sev.'

Straight ahead was a wide staircase. To the left and right, archways led into other rooms. MacFarlane was standing in the remains of the left-hand arch. MacRae followed him through. In the centre of the room was a pile of debris. MacRae knelt beside it and nodded at Rhona to bring the fire investigation kit.

'It smells like . . .' MacFarlane began.

'Don't bother, MacFarlane. You haven't the nose for it.'

MacRae filled the bag and handed it back to Rhona.

'Have they checked the windows?'

'All the ground floor ones were blown out with the blast,' MacFarlane told him. 'Gas and electricity have been off for the past year, so it wasn't a gas explosion.' He looked about. 'It'll be difficult to prove a break-in.'

A line of scorch marks was visible on the bare floorboards. Rhona followed it back to the archway.

'Don't wander about.' MacRae's voice followed her. 'Not until we're sure it's safe.'

'The fire ran this way.'

The scorch marks led to the foot of the staircase. Rhona wondered why she had missed them on her way in, but then her eyes had been on the ceiling, or what was left of it.

'I think someone piled bits of old shop fittings where you are now and splashed petrol about, then dripped it through here and up the stairs and back to the front door. When he lit it, the fire ran back into the side room.'

'Christ, MacFarlane, tell her!' The voice was sharp with exasperation.

Rhona noted MacFarlane's concerned face before she started up the stairs, but she had wanted to be sure. The first and second steps were burned through but the third and fourth showed the signs she was looking for.

'He's right,' MacFarlane tried.

'The petrol had already vaporised, that's what caused the explosion,' she looked back at them pleased.

'Shit!' MacRae was coming towards her but she was too engrossed in her explanation to care.

'The chemical reaction absorbed the majority of oxygen in the atmosphere so the fire . . .'

'Watch out!'

MacRae pulled her down the stairs and into the relative shelter of the archway as a section of ceiling gave way.

She would have apologised if he'd given her the chance but as soon as the noise stopped he headed for the entrance. MacFarlane shot her a look that suggested it would be better to keep her mouth shut, and followed MacRae out.

He was already dishing out orders.

'We need a scaffolding gantry before we put a full team in. No one, I repeat, no one, is to go back in there until we're sure of the ceiling. And MacFarlane, this is an old building. I bet most of the joists survived the fire. I'd like a proper look at them once the place is cleared.'

MacFarlane moved off towards the police tent, throwing Rhona an encouraging look as he left.

'So, what do we do now?' she asked MacRae.

'I wait until they make it safe.'

Rhona ignored the singular pronoun.

'How long will that take?'

His voice was clipped. 'Twenty-four hours, maybe more.'

She held up the sample bag. 'I'll send this to the lab. Get them to check for an agent.'

'Suit yourself.' He turned away.

'You think it was petrol?'

'I know it was.'

'You can't be sure until it's tested.'

'Look, lady . . .'

'My name's Rhona.'

'You play around with your chemical reactions all you like. That fire didn't just happen. Someone made it happen and that someone made it big and powerful enough to blow a young girl halfway across Princes Street.'

The *Big Issue* seller from Waverley was hovering on the edge of their conversation. An Alsatian stood alert beside him, looking like a police dog awaiting a command. On their right, MacFarlane emerged from the operations tent with a mobile held to his ear.

'MacFarlane!'

In broad daylight, MacFarlane looked worse than Rhona felt. He had probably been up all night.

'Who's the guy?' MacRae motioned behind him.

'Where?' The DI's tiredness was turning to stupidity.

'With the dog.'

'Oh, him. Name's Jaz. He knew the victim. That's her dog. He ran off with it, then changed his mind and came back. He offered to identify the body for us, while we try and find her family.'

MacRae turned. 'Come here, son.'

Jaz hesitated.

'Does the dog like chips?'

'Salt and sauce?'

'Of course.'

MacRae opened the Saab door. He grabbed a chip poke from the passenger seat and emptied its contents onto the road.

Emps looked up at Jaz.

'Go on!'

They watched as the dog devoured the chips, licking up the sauce like a pro.

'DI MacFarlane here says you knew the girl.'

'Karen didn't really know anybody. She liked to be

alone, except for Emperor. I spoke to her now and again. Offered her food. She never took it. She wouldn't beg either. She played the penny whistle for money. Rose Street mainly . . . she was good.'

Rhona bent and rubbed the dog's ears.

'Had Karen been sleeping round behind the hoarding?' she asked.

'I don't know. She could have been.' Jaz looked straight at Rhona. 'You think somebody started that fire deliberately, don't you?'

Rhona glanced at MacRae, but he said nothing.

'We don't know that yet.'

'That's murder.' The boy's voice was angry and the dog's head came up, neck hair bristling.

'Have you seen anyone hanging about the building?' Rhona asked.

He shook his head.

'We'll be back tomorrow. If you think of something you could speak to us then.'

The boy nodded and walked away, the dog at his heels.

MacRae was climbing back into the car. She asked where he was going. It was like a red rag to a bull.

'You're beginning to sound like my ex-wife. Correction, my estranged wife. For your information, I'm going to the scene of the last fire. The one that gave Gallagher a heart attack and landed me with you.'

Rhona kept her voice calm. He was not going to get her as rattled as he was. 'I'd like to come.'

'Suit yourself.'

The dog's chips weren't the only fast food in the car.

Rhona swept the remains of three other fish suppers onto the floor before getting in. The stereo was blasting out an old Marvin Gaye number. MacRae reached across and turned it up even louder.

Rhona kept her eyes on the road. Once you got used to the level, the music was alright. All those songs that sink into your brain so that years later you find yourself mouthing words you never knew you knew.

MacRae's face was as tired as MacFarlane's. Or else he had a hangover. Probably chronic. He drove like a maniac.

Ten minutes later they reached a burned-out office block.

'When did this happen?'

'Thursday last week.' He waved at the approaching security guard, who nodded and unlocked the entrance chain. MacRae held the temporary door to one side and Rhona stepped in. She was in a large, domed entrance hall. Ahead of her, a broad stairway spiralled upwards to a further two floors.

'It used to be a town house, then offices. Some computer consultancy firm had the first floor. An investment company had the top and the ground was an advertising company.'

'It must have been beautiful. That staircase especially.'

Despite the damage, the hall retained an elegance, its marble flooring blackened but intact.

'Can we use the stairs?'

'Not if you want to live.'

Behind the staircase a ladder had been erected through to the upper level. He motioned her to go first.

'Better you land on me, than me on you.'

Rhona wasn't convinced that was the only reason for the chivalry.

When she was halfway up he followed. She waited for him at the top. This time she wasn't going to wander.

He pointed at a pile of debris to the left of the door.

'He started it where we came up, burning a hole through the ceiling, then spread the accelerant out the door and down your nice staircase.'

'An insurance job?'

'The insurance company doesn't think so. The building was in the process of being sold for a good price. There was planning permission to convert it into flats.'

'Vandals?'

'I don't think so.'

MacRae went back down the ladder first, then watched her descent with interest. Wearing a skirt had been a bad choice, Rhona thought.

They walked back to the car.

'Any chance we could give the music a miss this time?'

The grin took her by surprise. MacRae looked completely different when he smiled.

'That bad?'

'That loud,' she said, returning his smile.

He switched off the stereo and started the car. This time the pace was slower.

'What does MacFarlane think about the fires?'

'MacFarlane thinks we have a nutter on our hands.'

'And you?'

The smile had gone. 'I don't know why the places were torched, but I'd risk my neck and say they were torched by the same person or persons. The jobs are professional. Same level of organisation and sophistication.'

'Do you have any idea who it might be?'

He reached across her and for a moment she thought he was going to turn on the stereo again. Instead he opened the glove compartment, brought out a letter and tossed it in her lap.

'This arrived this morning, delivered by hand to my flat.'

She opened it and read it. 'Whoever wrote this doesn't like you very much.'

'He likes women even less.'

Threatening letters were notoriously difficult to trace. It could take weeks, months of police time. In most cases the threat never materialised anyway. Frightening the recipient was usually enough for the letter-writer.

Rhona held the paper up to the light. Something had been spilt on it. She sniffed.

'Semen?'

'I would say so.'

Leaving evidence lying like this in a glove compartment with a half drunk bottle of whisky wasn't a good idea. She told him so. 'You should have given this to Forensic.'

'I just have.'

She held her tongue. She was beginning to learn confrontation didn't work with MacRae.

'I'll have it DNA sampled. We might get a match.'

He shook his head. 'If he was on file, he wouldn't have sent it.'

He might be right. DNA fingerprinting had become common knowledge, thanks to television.

She thought for a moment. 'The person who sent this may not be the one lighting the fires.'

His face was stubborn. 'He is.'

'Just once, you might be wrong.'

He was adamant. 'Not this time.'

They drove to his office in silence. At first glance, Rhona thought, there was no evidence to suggest the fires in the two cities were connected. Here, prominent buildings had been set on fire, not rundown council housing. If the fire-raiser had written that letter, then there was both a sexual element to his crimes and a desire to persecute and outwit the fire investigation team, ie MacRae. She glanced sideways. MacRae was obviously under a lot of pressure, and not just from the job. He was edgy, irritable and, judging from the bottle in the glove compartment, drinking too much. But he did have years of experience of fire investigation. She might be skilled in forensics, but he, like all fire investigators, had worked his way up from the ranks. He had fought numerous fires. He knew how they behaved.

MacRae's office was on the third floor of the red sandstone building that housed the headquarters of

Lothian and Borders Fire Brigade. The receptionist smiled at MacRae and gave Rhona the once-over.

'Any calls?'

'DI MacFarlane. Half an hour ago,' she told him.

They passed a display of old fire equipment and climbed the stairs. MacRae's office was small, with a desk, a filing cabinet and two easy chairs, both piled with papers. MacRae lifted a pile and motioned Rhona to sit down, then disappeared into the back room. On the desk, alongside three empty coffee cups, stood a photograph of a pretty, dark-haired woman and a girl of about six. Rhona wondered what had caused the separation and whether MacRae's drinking and chauvinistic attitude were the result or the cause.

MacRae called from the back room.

'Take a look in the top drawer of the filing cabinet, under miscellaneous.'

She pulled open the drawer. There were, at a guess, a dozen other letters. If these had anything to do with this investigation, then MacRae had been withholding evidence.

He was standing at the door, bare-chested, with a package in his hand. He tore the plastic wrapper off the new shirt and shook it loose.

'Does Gallagher know about these?' she asked, annoyed.

'I didn't want to be the one responsible for another heart attack.'

'That's not funny.'

'Who's laughing?'

MacRae turned away and Rhona's breath caught in

her throat. She had never seen such a badly burned body before, at least not one that had survived. Even the deep tan couldn't disguise the mass of mottled tissue that stretched from shoulder to shoulder.

Rhona forced herself to speak.

'You should have given these letters to Forensic,' she said.

MacRae was buttoning up the shirt. If he had sensed her reaction to his back, he chose to ignore it.

'We had that conversation, remember? Anyway, they're not all from the same bloke.' He shrugged. 'People don't like me prying into their fires. I might worry the insurance company enough not to pay out. So they write me letters.'

'They threaten you?'

'Some do. Others claim to have started the fire or think the fire was a sign of God's wrath.' He reached for a tie from the back of the chair. 'Take the letters with you if you like. They make good bedtime reading. See if you can pick out the ones from our friend, the wanker.'

He was putting on his jacket. 'MacFarlane said you were staying over. Can I ask where?'

'With a friend.'

'Male?'

'I don't see . . .'

'Easy. You can stay with a transvestite poodle for all I care. Provided it has a loud bark.'

He had come right up to her. She could smell the pressed cotton of the new shirt.

'What do you mean?'

'The arsonist sees us as the enemy. For the moment he's outwitting us. If he thinks we're getting too close . . .'

She interrupted him. 'I've only been here a day.'

'Long enough.'

He headed for the door. 'If you want a lift, we have to go now. I have a date and I'm late already.'

The traffic was heavy in the city centre but MacRae dodged through it, oblivious to angry shouts and blasting horns. Rhona began to wish she had taken a taxi. She suggested he could drop her at the west end of Princes Street and she would find her own way to Greg's flat from there.

'I'll take you right to the door after I pick up my date,' was the curt reply.

Whoever the woman was, MacRae didn't want to be late for her. And she had been feeling sorry for him because he was separated from his wife and family!

They reached the house ten minutes later. MacRae sounded the horn and Rhona caught sight of a figure at the window, then the door opened and the wee girl in the photograph came running down the path.

The child waited until MacRae rolled down the window then gave him a good telling-off.

'You're late and Mum's angry.'

MacRae's wife was following her daughter.

'Amy's been ready for half an hour,' she said sharply.

'It's okay, Gillian, we've got plenty of time. The film doesn't start till 5.30.' He turned to Amy who was

settling herself happily in the back seat. 'Amy, this is
Dr MacLeod. She's helping me while Mr Gallagher's
in hospital.'

'Hello, Dr MacLeod.'

'Hello, Amy.'

'You didn't say anyone else was going.'

The suggestion was all too obvious.

'I'm not going to the film, Mrs MacRae.' Rhona
hoped she didn't sound as embarrassed as she felt. 'Mr
MacRae just offered me a lift back to my flat.'

'Did he?'

MacRae was rolling up the window. 'I'll have Amy
back by eight.'

'You'd better.'

The only one who talked on the way to Greg's was
Amy. She chatted on about school, her best friend
Katie and her pet hamster.

Rhona sat seething. MacRae had deliberately misled
her into thinking he was meeting a woman when he was
collecting his child. Then he deliberately embarrassed
her by making his wife think he was going out with her.
The fact that she knew she was exaggerating the
situation didn't make any difference. One thing was
sure. MacRae couldn't care less about other people's
feelings.

The journey took too long for Rhona and when they
got there she had to endure the expression on Mac-
Rae's face as he looked up at the luxury block.

'Isn't this the street where a flat went for half a
million recently?'

'I have no idea.'

'Quite a catch.'

'Greg is gay,' Rhona said defensively.

She got out and shut the door.

'I'll see you tomorrow.'

'Sure.'

She turned to go.

'Are you eating out?' The cynical tone had gone.

'Why?'

'Stay clear of the Italian on the corner. It's over-priced and the food's crap. And take your gay friend with you. For safety's sake.'

7

THE FLAT WAS empty, but Greg had left the hall light on and there was a note from him beside the phone.

Make yourself at home. There's food in the fridge but if you can't be bothered cooking, there's an Italian on the corner.

Rhona went into the spare room. She emptied her bag on the bed, grabbed her dressing-gown and shampoo and headed for the shower.

She didn't hear the phone at first. When she did, she assumed Greg's ansaphone would click on, but it didn't and the phone went on ringing. She climbed out of the shower and grabbed a towel.

The line clicked dead as soon as she said hello. Rhona tried 1471 but the number had been withheld.

She thought for a moment, then threw the bolt on the front door and unbolted it again seconds later. She would not let Severino MacRae unnerve her.

She was halfway through drying her hair when the phone rang again. She was there on the third ring.

'Who is it?' she shouted.

'Hey. Take it easy.' It was Chrissy.

'Sorry. I had the hairdryer on. It deafens me.'

'You sound more like pissed off. Bad day?'

'I've had better.'

'The samples arrived. I sent most of them to Chemistry,' Chrissy said accusingly.

'I'm sending through a letter . . .'

'Not handwriting analysis?'

Chrissy's voice was a mixture of disappointment and cynicism. Handwriting specialists came a little lower than forensic chemists in Chrissy's scheme of things.

'I want you to look at it first,' Rhona said. 'It's impregnated with something.'

Chrissy was interested now. 'Blood? Perfume?'

'Possibly semen. Can you check it on the DNA database?'

'Sure. Bit of a long shot though.'

'I know. MacRae had other letters in his filing cabinet that Forensic haven't seen. Some of them may be from the same man. I want to read them, before I send them through. Anything on the Glasgow fire?'

'Are you familiar with thallium poisoning?'

'I've seen it once before. Why?'

'The victim was at the doctor's last week with a crop of symptoms that might have been caused by thallium poisoning. We're running some tests. I'll have more when you get back. When is that likely to be?'

'As soon as possible.'

The restaurant was too upmarket for Rhona, but it had been difficult to retreat. The young man at the desk gave her the once-over, then asked pointedly if there would be one or two persons eating. When she said one, he raised his eyebrows and escorted her to a corner table inches from the kitchen entrance. The other diners, mostly couples, glanced briefly in her direction then went back to their conversations.

Rhona wondered whether reading the forensic magazine she'd brought with her would make her more conspicuous, then decided it was better than staring into space. When the waiter arrived she ordered a pasta dish and a half bottle of house white. She was absorbed in an article about cocaine residue on American bank notes when she noticed MacRae standing at the entrance impatiently scanning the diners.

Rhona buried her face in her magazine, praying he wouldn't spot her.

No such luck.

He removed a chair from a nearby table and sat opposite her. 'I thought I told you not to eat here.'

Rhona avoided catching his eye. 'I don't think it's part of the job of the fire investigator to tell the forensic where to eat.'

'So you don't accept advice? Even from a expert?'

The waiter was offering MacRae a menu. He ignored it. Rhona shook her head and the waiter gave her a knowing look. Lovers' tiff, it said.

'So what's so important you came looking for me?' she asked, trying to be reasonable.

MacRae stood up. 'I'll explain on the way.'

'I can't just leave.' This was ridiculous. Did he think

he just had to call and she would follow him about like a pet dog?

'Why not?'

'I've not finished my wine.'

He reached for the bottle. 'We'll take it with us.'

'No.' She grabbed it back. 'I haven't paid for it yet. Anyway,' she topped up her glass, 'I've already ordered.'

'You've what?'

'Keep your voice down.'

'If you don't come,' he whispered dramatically, 'I'll be forced to tell all these people about the aubergines.'

'Don't be stupid.'

He shrugged and stood up. 'Ladies and gentlemen, I'm sorry to interrupt your meal but being from the Department of Public Health I feel it only fair to warn you about the sexual predilections of the current chef of this establishment, which involve aubergines . . .'

Rhona lifted her jacket from the back of the chair, left money on the table for the astonished waiter and headed for the door.

When MacRae opened the car, the music was on full blast. He turned it down before she got in. The chip pokes had gone.

'My daughter doesn't like an untidy car. Takes after her mother in that respect.'

Rhona ignored his attempts at conversation and looked pointedly out of the window. They had left the city centre and were heading north, towards the Forth. She refused to ask MacRae where he was taking her, but whatever he wanted her to see, it had better be good.

8

IT TOOK TEN minutes to get to the important place that had spoiled her dinner. On her right hand side was a small harbour, half a dozen boats beached on the mud. On her left a long, low white building with bright red signs. Rhona stared out of the window in disbelief.

'What's this?'

'A *real* restaurant. Best fish and chips in Edinburgh.' MacRae was actually grinning at her. 'It's impossible to get a table here on a Friday night. Ian promised to hold one for fifteen minutes, no more.'

'This is why you embarrassed me and dragged me from my meal?'

MacRae shrugged his shoulders. 'It got you here, didn't it?'

He was already out of the car.

'Come on. I've removed you from hell and taken you to heaven. What more do you want?'

The smile MacRae got from the waitress was verging on a come-on. She twinkled and bobbed and escorted them to their table with a swing of her hips.

'Amy likes it here,' said MacRae, handing Rhona the menu. 'They make a fuss of her.'

'They make a fuss of her father too.'

For the first time MacRae looked embarrassed, but the look disappeared so quickly Rhona wondered if she'd imagined it.

'Okay, what is it you wanted to show me?' she insisted.

'After you sample some real fish and chips.'

Rhona refilled her cup from the large teapot and sat back in the chair. MacRae had been in the kitchen for the past five minutes. As he disappeared through the doors he had been greeted with cries of welcome. It made her think. MacRae was different tonight. Seeing his daughter had done him good. This morning he had been coiled and tense. Tonight he was relaxed.

He emerged, laughing. Behind him a handsome male face grinned out.

'Jamie sends his love.' MacRae sat down. 'I told him you're not interested.'

'What makes you think that?'

'No time,' he smiled, 'or was it no inclination?'

He held her eyes until she looked away.

'Why did you bring me here?'

His face grew serious.

'This was on my windscreen when I came out of the cinema.'

He handed her a typed note.

She read out the words. 'I hope you'll be at the party?'

MacRae's face confirmed her suspicions.

'He means the Hogmanay street party, doesn't he?'

'The arsonist profiles as power-assertive. He achieves a sense of superiority through expressing exploitative control, dominance and intrusive violations of the law. In layman's terms, he gets his kicks from mayhem. With the crowds that'll turn out over New Year, he'll have his biggest audience to date.'

'You're certain the fires weren't insurance or fraud jobs?'

'If a building is set on fire for insurance purposes, no one lets us know, before or after the event.'

If the person responsible for the fires had no more reason for lighting them than pleasure, it would make him almost impossible to catch.

MacRae was reading her mind. 'The worst kind to find.'

The ring of his mobile broke the silence that followed. As he listened to the caller, his expression became fraught with worry.

'I'm on my way.'

He was on his feet.

'What's wrong?'

His voice was hardly more than a whisper.

'Someone threw a petrol bomb through Amy's bedroom window.'

MacRae ignored the No Waiting sign and the double yellow lines and swept into an ambulance space outside Casualty. It had taken twenty minutes to get to the hospital. MacRae had ignored every red light and kept his horn on full blast most of the way. Rhona had expected a police car to stop them at any time. When she offered to park the car, MacRae threw the keys in her lap without speaking.

Rhona sat for a while in the car park trying to decide whether to go in to the hospital or not. She desperately wanted to know if Amy was okay, but if Gillian was there it would look bad. She didn't want to cause any trouble between MacRae and his wife, especially now.

When she entered reception, MacRae was standing alone, but almost immediately the lift door opened and Gillian emerged. Rhona waited at the entrance but MacRae caught sight of her and motioned her over.

The words were tumbling out of Gillian.

'Amy was in bed. She was tired after the cinema. I heard a crash, then Amy screaming. By the time I got to her the room was full of smoke. I got her downstairs and outside. Mr Fraser next door phoned the Fire Brigade.'

'Where's Amy?'

'Ward 7. She'll be alright.' Her relief was inflected with anger. 'I knew something like this would happen but you would never believe the threats. The job always came first.'

MacRae's knuckles were clenched white.

'This isn't the time to discuss my job.'

'Your job almost killed our daughter.'

MacRae looked stricken.

'Gillian, please . . . why don't you and Amy come back and stay with me in the flat?'

Gillian was staring at Rhona.

'Wouldn't that be a little crowded?'

MacRae looked weary. 'Dr MacLeod is covering

Gallagher's job. She's staying at a friend's flat, not mine.'

Gillian was unconvinced.

'*You* threw *me* out, Gillian. Remember?'

'It seems throwing you out wasn't enough.'

MacRae turned to Rhona. 'I'm going to see Amy. Can you take a taxi back?'

She nodded. 'Of course.'

Gillian threw Rhona a look as MacRae entered the lift. Rhona wondered if her presumption of infidelity was based on past experience. Or was it the sense that she could never come before the job in Severino's life?

9

JAZ COULDN'T SLEEP. He rolled out of bed and went to stand at the window. The lights of Edinburgh stared back at him. He had been in this flat for three months and he still loved it with a passion he would have found impossible to describe. The only people who could ever understand what this flat meant to him had been homeless themselves.

He left the window and went into the tiny kitchenette, filled the kettle and popped a tea-bag into a cup. He didn't bother with milk. Without a fridge it went off too quickly. He scooped two teaspoonfuls of sugar into the cup and poured in the boiling water.

The dog was awake and when Jaz sat down it came and laid its head in his lap. Emperor was missing Karen. Every time he heard a female voice on the stairs, he was up and at the door.

Jaz was the same, even though Karen had never been in the flat. He'd offered her a bed one night when it was really cold, but she'd refused.

'Emps keeps me warm,' she told him.

He'd gone back with the dog and the policeman had taken a note of his address and told him he could hang on to Emps for now. Jaz had offered to look at the body, check if it was Karen. They'd agreed because they knew it would take time to locate a relative, if they managed at all. Kids like Karen were running from someone or something, and it wasn't usually concerned families.

The blast had hit her back, so her face was recognisable. It only took a second but the smell of burnt flesh stayed in his nostrils. That and a terrible feeling of anger.

It wouldn't be light for another hour. Jaz rinsed his cup at the sink. It was a good time to find the people he needed to talk to. The ones who might have seen someone hanging about the empty building. The people nobody noticed or if they did they looked straight ahead and pretended they hadn't. The people who were an embarrassment to the good folks of Edinburgh. People like him.

Outside the streets were glistening in a light frost. Jaz stuck his hands in his pockets, whistled lightly to Emps to follow and set off for the Grassmarket.

To the tourists, the Grassmarket meant pubs and eateries. To Jaz, the down-and-outs who sat begging from passers-by gave the place its character. At night they clogged the alleys and jammed the doorways. These were the long-stay patrons of Edinburgh's underbelly; the ex-servicemen whose lives had fallen apart, the drunks and the addicts.

Traffic was beginning to flow along Chambers Street as he passed the Museum of Scotland and headed down by Greyfriars churchyard to the Cowgate. The men's hostel on the corner was closed but there was an old guy coughing up spit on the front steps. Jaz recognised him.

The Bruce wasn't one to miss a chance. He had his hand out right away.

'Any change, Mister?'

Jaz dropped a pound coin plus fifty pence in the dirty palm and the face lit up. The price of a can of extra-strong lager. Breakfast had arrived.

'Ah, you're alright son.'

'It's me. Jaz.'

The old guy's face worked hard on focusing.

'I'm looking for Mary,' Jaz explained.

The face changed to suspicion. 'What d'you want the Queen for?'

'I need to talk to her.'

'The Queen doesn't talk. Not sense anyway.'

The old guy was shuffling off towards a High Street newsagent and off-licence open early enough for breakfast. Jaz walked beside him.

'I heard Mary had a little trouble.'

'What's it to you?'

They were nearing the shop. There was anticipation in the old man's step. In his head he was already swallowing the lager, feeling the surge as the alcohol met his brain. He might be a drunk, but he was shrewd. If Jaz wanted information, he would pay for it.

The owner was pulling up the safety grille, lifting the big bags of delivered rolls from the shop doorway.

'We could buy four cans and a couple of rolls,' Jaz said. 'Keep you going for a while.'

The old guy was summing up the offer. 'Forget the fuckin' rolls and make it six cans.'

Jaz nodded. It would skin him, but he needed to talk to Mary. If what he'd heard was true, she might know who lit the fire.

The Bruce waited till the money was across the counter and the pack of lager in his hands.

'The Queen's in the Infirmary. Some bastard tried to get her out of a squat. She wouldn't budge, so he set her hair alight.'

'Was it the same guy she told the Wallace about?'

'The same one.' The Bruce laughed. 'Stupid bitch is cracking up. No drink allowed in the hospital.' His laugh sounded like dirty water going down a blocked drain. 'She wants the Wallace and me to rescue her.' Then he was off across the road to a wooden bench.

There was no point turning up at the hospital until nearer official visiting time. If Queen Mary knew anything, he would find out soon enough. Jaz headed for his pitch outside Waverley, turning over in his mind what he should do after that. All he knew was that Karen shouldn't have died. Whoever lit that fire was responsible for her death. If the police didn't find him, he would do it himself.

10

'WE FOUND A leather pouch round her waist. The pocket was at the front so it escaped much of the heat. It held some coins . . . and this.'

Dr MacKenzie handed Rhona a photograph. The bright young face stared out at her, side by side with the Alsatian. Rhona wondered how the girl had persuaded the dog into the booth, then made it sit in such a way they were both visible for the flash. The dog's tongue hung out, long and pink and dripping. It had a grin on to match its mistress's.

'She had just about enough money for her next meal, a penny whistle and a change of clothing, plus the remains of the tartan blanket.' The pathologist nodded to the bagged items behind him. 'According to eye-witnesses, the blast from the backdraft was extensive. From the state of the body, she must have been facing away from the fire, but directly in its path. The lacerations to the back of the skull suggest intense heat. Her front is relatively unmarked except for the genital area.'

'What do you mean?'

He motioned her forward.

'The pubic hair is burned away, the genitals blistered, yet this area would have been shielded from the blast.'

'Do you mean these burns were inflicted before the explosion?'

He nodded. If that was true, it was the first link between the Glasgow fire and this one.

'I take it you want to stay while we open her up?'

Rhona nodded.

The doctor reached for an array of instruments beside him. Each pathologist had his own systematic procedure for post-mortem. Rhona watched as Dr MacKenzie chose the favoured way, a simple incision down the middle of the body from the neck to the pubis, making a detour round the tougher skin of the navel.

'The usual samples have already gone to the lab,' he said. 'You may speak to my assistant about those if you wish. Apart from the genital burns, there is no suggestion of violent injury prior to death. However, there was evidence of recent sexual contact, which may or may not have been consensual.' He paused as he lifted the stomach clear of the body and manoeuvred it over a container. 'And if I'm not mistaken, nothing to eat for some time.'

The scissors bit through the stomach wall, releasing the meagre contents into the container with a soft plop.

The girl had been living on fresh air. Whatever she had earned from playing the whistle had not been spent on food.

'Maybe she was feeding a habit?' Rhona suggested.

'More likely feeding the dog. A dog that size needs

copious amounts of food and seeing it tied up outside the tent, it was well looked after. Anyway, we'll know about drugs once we get the results of the urine tests.'

'She was very young,' Rhona said, thinking about the face in the picture.

'I would suggest a little over fifteen. The breasts are small and not, I think, fully formed. We'll be able to tell from the hair samples, but I'm fairly sure she hadn't reached late teens.'

'Jaz, the boy who took her dog, said she had no family.' It hardly seemed possible that a fifteen-year-old girl could be sleeping rough on the streets of their capital city and no one had reported her missing.

Dr MacKenzie's tone was tart. 'I take it there are no homeless girls on the streets of Glasgow?'

'They don't usually make their living playing the penny whistle,' Rhona said.

'This one may not have either if the semen is anything to go by.'

'I'd like to check your DNA findings against a seminal fluid sample we have already.'

'Of course.'

Rhona was glad to leave the sterile atmosphere of the Pathology Lab and breathe in Edinburgh's pollution instead. She stood on the steps outside, clearing her head of the scent of death. The police car was waiting at the kerb. She would pick up her things and head back to Glasgow. The message from her lab via Mac-Farlane had simply stated she was needed.

She thought briefly about calling the hospital to

check on Amy then decided against it. If Gillian was there, it might make things worse. Judging by Gillian's reaction the previous night, it was time for MacRae to choose between his family and his work.

When or if she returned to Edinburgh, the chances were she would find herself working with someone other than Severino MacRae. Rhona was surprised by her sudden feeling of disappointment and quickly dismissed it. She didn't like working with MacRae and he didn't like working with her. It would be easier for both of them if the investigation passed to someone else. But what if the warning on the windscreen was for real?

Hogmanay tourists thronged the north side of Princes Street, ambling in and out of souvenir shops, stopping to take pictures of the castle. Traffic was flowing again, the incident tent was down. To her left the shattered building was a hive of activity. The scaffolding was up and a team at work inside. A white suit emerged as the police car passed, face encased in a cartridge respirator. MacRae wasn't taking any chances. Buildings like these were often lined with asbestos, and sifting through the debris risked disturbing particles of the lethal substance. Then there were the noxious gases trapped under deposits which might be released during excavation.

The car rolled down the ramp into Waverley station.

'Mr MacRae said he'll call you later,' the driver told her.

'I didn't tell Mr MacRae I had to go back to Glasgow,' she said, puzzled.

'He asked me to give you this.'

The driver handed Rhona a brown envelope with 'for the Lady Scientist' scrawled roughly over it.

Rhona settled herself in a window seat. The train was quiet. It wasn't a peak time for travelling between the two cities. She placed the envelope face up on the table in front of her and for once the title 'Lady' didn't irritate her. She wondered what effect the contents of the envelope would have.

After returning from the hospital, she'd read through the bundle of letters from MacRae's filing cabinet. When Greg arrived back around two she was still up, mulling over them. Some were general complaints and acts of God. Four looked as though they came from 'the wanker', as MacRae called him. The front door opening and muffled laughter from the hall had broken into her thoughts. Greg stuck his head round her bedroom door, his eyes hazy with drink.

'Didn't think you'd be awake. I've brought someone back with me. Hope you don't mind?'

'Of course not.'

'We won't make a noise,' he promised.

He was true to his word. Either the walls were soundproof or it was the quietest lovemaking on the planet. Rhona turned up the stereo to stop herself thinking about sex.

It was the sight and smell of death that did it. Rhona had experienced the feeling many times before. The need to prove to herself that she was alive to shake off the presence of death.

She picked up the four separate letters and laid them one by one across the bed.

Fire aroused the arsonist. Made him feel alive, when nothing else could. But this wasn't a roll on the rug in front of a log fire. His fires had caused devastation on a grand scale, and now death.

The sound of traffic outside had dwindled to an occasional hum. Rhona rose and stood at the window, wishing Sean would call her. She desperately wanted to hear his voice. No. She wanted his weight on her, his breath in her hair. She wanted the smell of sex in her nostrils.

The street was deserted, save for a man with a dog. The figure paused and looked up and Rhona strained to make out the face in the orange glow of the street light. The dog lifted its leg and marked the lamp post, then with a small yelp urged its master on.

11

'WHAT THE HELL is going on, MacFarlane?'

'Take it easy, Sev. We're on the case. All known punks . . .' MacFarlane didn't get to finish. Severino threw the electric razor on the desk. Shaving hadn't made him look any better. Bed and sleep were both an elusive dream.

'Cut the crap. You and I both know who did it.'

'We don't know for certain,' MacFarlane countered.

'Correction. This arrived this morning.' Severino threw an envelope across the desk. 'The bastard knows everything about me and our lady forensic. Gillian's talking about taking Amy north to her mother's. As far away from me as possible.'

MacFarlane said: 'I'm sorry.'

Severino paused before the next barb. It wasn't MacFarlane's fault. He was doing his best. But it wasn't enough. If it were just himself, it would be different. But not Amy.

'Look, I investigate fires. I'm not responsible for finding the people who set them. That's your job.'

'If he hits during the street party we have to be ready for him.'

'You're talking to the wrong man, MacFarlane,' he said firmly. 'You want fire *prevention.*'

The DI wasn't giving up. 'There will be a lot of people about.'

MacFarlane was putting words to the pictures in Sev's own head.

'Cancel the celebrations. You would cancel for a terrorist threat. Edinburgh's become fireworks city. It thinks it's fucking Disneyland.'

'You know we can't do that. Not on what we have.' MacFarlane looked apologetic. 'The three days are a sell-out. Sky's covering the whole event.'

Sev shrugged his shoulders.

'Suit yourself. It's nothing to do with me.'

'But you know how he thinks.' MacFarlane was like a dog with a bone.

'In case you haven't noticed,' Sev said, 'I always get there after the event.'

'He's never warned us before.'

Sev ran his hand through his hair. It didn't help his brain. He had gone over the same idea a hundred times. It still didn't fit.

'Has it never occurred to you that's what's wrong?'

In the distance the castle dominated the skyline, Union Jack fluttering in the breeze. Her Majesty's garrison in Scotland. If the bastard had his mind set on the city centre, the castle might be the only safe place this weekend.

'While we all run round trying to figure out if, where and when during the Hogmanay party he's going to perform,' he went on grimly, 'the bastard will be somewhere else.'

'We have to take that chance.'

'No. You have to take that chance.' Sev picked up a buff folder. 'Here's my report.' He shoved it in Mac-Farlane's face. 'The last four fires in the city centre have been started deliberately, I believe by the same person or persons. All the details are there.'

He turned to leave.

'Where are you going?'

'A drink, home and bed. In that order.'

His jacket was behind the door. MacRae pulled it off the hook, slung it over his shoulder and swung round. He wanted to be sure of one thing before he left.

'She got the message?'

'She was on the twelve o'clock to Glasgow. I'll make sure she doesn't come back.'

'Thanks.'

MacFarlane looked gloomily resigned: 'She'll be safer in Glasgow.'

'We'd all be safer in Glasgow.'

12

SEV DIDN'T LOOK up when Jaz entered the bar. Instead he drained his whisky glass and waved it for a refill. He wasn't in the mood to talk to anyone, least of all him.

When he left the office, he'd made for the centre of town rather than the flat. There was no need to visit the fire scene again. He'd signed off. He'd kept his promise to Gillian. But it wasn't Gillian's frightened demands the night before that had made up his mind. It was standing in the ward looking at Amy's pale face, the dark shadows under her eyes. His wee girl. She was okay, they'd told him. She was being kept in overnight only as a precaution. That hadn't made him feel any better.

The whisky slid down his throat and bit at his chest. It numbed his thoughts but it didn't drown them out. When he'd arrived at the building this morning, his whole team had known about what had happened at Gillian's. He could tell by their faces, the dropped looks, the caution in the voices. He had ignored it all and they'd got started, glad not to have to say anything. They would systematically comb the debris, bit by bit, just as he had told them. But it was probably all a complete waste of time. While they were tied up analysing this job, the arsonist would be planning his next strike.

Jaz was standing behind him. He heard the scuffle of the dog's claws on the floor as it sat at the boy's command.

'Hey.'

Sev turned. 'Hey.' He patted the dog and it licked his hand.

'Buy you a drink?'

'No thanks.'

'Not your drug, eh?'

Jaz ignored the taunt.

'Have you found out who it was that killed Karen?'

'You're talking to the wrong man,' Sev heard himself say. 'You want DI MacFarlane of Lothian and Borders Police.'

'What if the same guy hurt your little girl?'

Sev grabbed him by the jacket. Jaz didn't resist. His back pressed against the counter, he stared at Sev, his eyes accusing.

'Who told you that?' Sev tightened his grip. The dog growled.

Suddenly Sev's anger drained as quickly as it had erupted. He loosened his hold and Jaz stumbled free.

Sev picked up his glass, his hand shaking. He was losing it, he realised with a flash of clarity. The image of Amy's face in that hospital bed kept swamping his mind. The thought that she could have been badly burned, or worse still, lying in a coffin, made him sick with fear.

'Go away,' he said brusquely.

But this one was as stubborn as MacFarlane.

'Don't you want to nail the bastard?' Jaz said.

'I'll nail him with my evidence,' Sev said quietly.

'You have to catch him first.'

The guy was like a fly buzzing round his head. Swatting him hadn't worked. What now? Sev looked Jaz up and down. The ponytail, the combat gear, the big boots, the determined face.

'I know who he is.'

'What?'

'A mate of mine, Mary Queen of Scots, hangs about the Gardens with two old guys, the Bruce and the Wallace . . .'

That was all he needed. The demented drunken ravings of resurrected Scottish heroes. Sev stopped him mid-sentence. 'Alkies.' He waved at the barman for a refill.

Jaz slid his eyes pointedly to the glass. Sev got the message.

Jaz went on: 'This guy told Mary to move from her squat last Friday night or he'd torch her. He came back when she was asleep and set her hair alight. The Wallace and the Bruce heard her screaming. The hospital kept her in for a week and she didn't get any drink . . .'

'I can sympathise with that.'

The boy ignored the cynical remark. 'She's been on the bevvy ever since,' he went on. 'She's shit-scared he'll come back and get her.'

'Maybe this guy just doesn't like smelly old alkies squatting in his building.'

'He isn't the owner.'

Sev knew he should stop listening now. Tell the boy to take his story to MacFarlane, keep out of it. But the story was planting itself in his brain, burrowing down.

'So where's this building, then?' he asked finally.

'I wrote down the address.' Jaz pulled a piece of paper from his pocket and flattened it on the counter.

Below the address was a pencil drawing of a face.

'What's this?'

'Mary described the guy, so I drew him. It took a few tries, but she swears this looks just like him. And she might be an alkie, but she never forgets a face.' The boy's voice was anxious.

Sev examined the drawing. It was impossible to know if it caught a likeness, but if it did, he would know this face again. 'You *are* a wee smart-arse.'

The boy looked pleased. 'He's about heights with me. Twenties. She says he smells nice.'

Sev looked him up and down. 'Not on the streets then?'

'You don't smell so sweet yourself.' Jaz was giving as good as he got.

'I've been up all night.'

'At least you've got a bed to go to.'

Sev nodded at the picture. 'Can I keep this?'

'If you like. I've got a spare.'

He folded the sketch and put it in his pocket, then put some money on the counter for his drinks. Jaz was watching him. Sev suddenly remembered what the pathologist had said when he phoned about the post-mortem. The dead girl had been living on fresh air.

'You hungry?'

The chin was up, defensive and proud. 'I don't need your money.'

MacRae looked down at the dog. 'Buy my friend some chips then.' He pushed some change across the counter. 'And don't forget the salt and sauce.'

13

CHRISSY LOOKED UP from the forensic journal.

'It says here that one gram of thallium sulphate constitutes a lethal dose in an adult. With doses greater than two grams, the illness progresses rapidly to cardiovascular shock, coma and death within 24 hours.'

'If someone wanted rid of him, why not give him a straightforward overdose?', Rhona suggested.

Chrissy shrugged. 'A waste of good cocaine?' She slammed the book shut. 'Neat stuff, eh? Colourless, tasteless and odourless. Found as a contaminant in some Chinese herbal medicines, rodenticide and green fireworks, can be mistaken for cocaine and sniffed . . .'

'What did you say?'

'I said lots of things. Which one?'

'You said something about fireworks.'

'Green fireworks. It's in green-emitting fireworks.'

Chrissy gave her a look that accused her mind of being elsewhere, which it was.

'Visited the drug centre a week before he died complaining of nausea, vomiting and abdominal pain,' Rhona read from the report. 'The doctor there reported him as manifesting acute nervous and gastro-intestinal symptoms. He wanted to admit him to hospital. He refused and was persuaded to give urine and blood samples. He then left.'

'One week later he's found dead of an apparent overdose in a burned out building,' Chrissy added.

'The general lab tests on the urine and blood showed nothing,' said Rhona thoughtfully, 'but then they weren't looking for thallium.'

'By the pricking of my thumbs, something wicked this way comes,' said Chrissy darkly.

Rhona laughed despite herself. 'I didn't know you were a Shakespearean scholar.'

'I'm not. It's from a Ray Bradbury book.' Chrissy shook her head. 'Let's face it. Something smells like shite.'

'You're sure about the hair?'

'Come and see for yourself,' Chrissy offered. 'Most of the hair was singed but I got some from the back of the head. Of course, we don't have a control sample from before death but . . .'

Under the polarised light, the dark bands and distorted anagen roots supported Chrissy's diagnosis of thallium poisoning. Rhona glanced up. 'The urine and blood taken after death?'

'We're working on that now.' Chrissy's self-satisfied tone suggested that life went on as usual even if the Captain had left the ship.

'I'd better call Bill.'

Bill wasn't mincing his words. 'They don't want you back.'

'Why not?' She tried to sound disinterested.

'Apparently you're difficult to work with.' He paused and when she didn't reply, felt safe to go on. 'Anyway,' he said placatingly, 'you've got your hands full here.'

Rhona came back at him. 'And you agreed?'

'It isn't up to me.'

'So what's to stop me going back?'

'Saving your sanity?' he suggested.

Bill was right. There was no reason to return. The samples from the Princes Street blaze had been tested and confirmed the use of an accelerant. They were still waiting on an exact breakdown but that would arrive soon. The presence of an accelerant was all they needed. The trawl on the DNA sample from the semen on the letter had revealed nothing. Neither had the semen left in the girl. And they didn't match.

'Did you speak to DI MacFarlane?' she asked.

'Yes. He suspects the arsonist will strike again soon.'

'So we just wait and see?' she said.

'*They* wait and see. *We* worry about our own.'

She should keep her nose out of the East's affairs. That was fine by her. There was plenty of work here without bailing out the East. She changed the subject to the Glasgow case.

'Chrissy's tests confirm Dr Sissons' suspicions about the presence of thallium in the body.'

'What the hell's that?'

'Thallium salts are colourless, tasteless and odourless,' Rhona explained. 'A poisoner's dream.'

'Where the hell would he get thallium?'

'Rodenticides, pesticides, Chinese medicines, fireworks. He could also have sniffed it thinking it was cocaine. Wherever he got it, it was a potentially lethal dose.'

Bill wasn't convinced. 'Cocaine would be a bit upmarket for him.'

'Well, if there's cocaine contaminated with thallium out there, there'll be more like him soon.'

'Great.'

'I suggest you warn the drop-in centres to look out for tell-tale signs. I'll send you a standard description to pass round.'

'Thanks.'

'And Bill, I think the blisters on the wrists happened before death. If the victim was being fed thallium and getting his wrists burned, someone didn't like him very much.'

'He wasn't a dealer as far as we know. Maybe he owed his supplier money?'

'Suppliers don't normally kill their customers. It cuts the profit margin.'

'Maybe we should check back over the last year. He wasn't the first junkie to die of an overdose in that area,' Bill said thoughtfully.

'Just what I was thinking.'

'Mind you, there was no reason to think about poisoning in the other cases.'

'There is now. And Bill?' she caught him before he rang off. 'Personally I'd like to know who's behind the redevelopment plans for that area. Junkies have a bad habit of lowering the tone of the neighbourhood.'

* * *

When she finally got round to attacking her desk, the contents suggested she had been away for a week rather than a couple of days. The report from Chemistry lay on top. Rhona checked through it again. Most forensic laboratories felt confident in identifying the commonly found accelerants like petrol and kerosene on the basis of their chromatograms alone. Spenser had gone one step further. The Edinburgh sample report was conclusive. But then, Severino MacRae had known that by his nose.

Rhona pulled the brown envelope from her briefcase and emptied its contents on the desk. The photographs of the Princes Street building only served to confirm the conclusions. The burning pattern was obvious, the seat of the fire revealed as she'd suggested. She was momentarily embarrassed by the memory of that morning in the burned-out building, her determination to tell the man his job. Still, she had been right and no more insufferable than MacRae himself.

She had a quick look through the remaining photographs. The wide-angle lens had been used to photograph the building from the two opposite corners, showing the overall degree of fire damage and the locations of the various entrances and windows. The aerial photograph showed the force of the explosion and the trail of debris that sprayed the railings and beyond. The photographer had taken two shots, once right above the building, one nearer the front covering the debris, the railings and the gardens. The white tent was already up round the body. Rhona winced when she spotted the flash of blue among the roses behind

the tent. So that was why MacRae had included this
one. He couldn't resist the parting shot. Forensic
Scientist being sick in the flowerbeds.

She checked the back in case he'd written a caption,
but it was blank. It was his idea of a joke. She shoved
the photographs to one side. Forty-six miles away, and
MacRae was still irritating her.

Rhona opened her inbox. There was an email from
Chemistry about their report, a couple from other
forensic labs, a request from a forensic student to visit
the lab. She opened each in turn, storing them in
folders for later action.

She kept Liam's email for last. She took a breath
then clicked it open, her heart thumping. The message
was short and to the point. He would call when he
knew what his movements were over the New Year. He
signed it simply 'L'.

Disappointment and relief swept over her. Liam was
as nervous as she was about meeting.

Rhona pulled her mind away from the subject of her
son and got wired into the job she liked least, the
paperwork. If she concentrated on her reports it would
stop her thinking about Edinburgh and about Liam.

When she pushed open her front door three hours
later, the flat smelt stuffy and unlived-in. She had
stopped on her way up the stairs and thanked Mrs
Harper for feeding the cat in her absence.

'My pleasure, dear. There's some post for you, I left
it on the hall table, and your ansaphone's blinking.'
Mrs Harper gave Rhona a knowing smile. She was one

of Sean's many admirers, and she took her vicarious mothering seriously.

Rhona shuffled through the bills and circulars, wishing that Sean wrote letters the way he wrote music. The most she could hope for when he was away would be a postcard.

She went in search of some alcohol and found an unexpected bottle of white wine in the door of the fridge. She was the one who bought white wine. Sean didn't like it. She tried to remember when she'd bought it, and couldn't. She carried her filled glass to the hall and sat down to listen to the phone messages. When the tune began, Rhona thought the caller had the radio on too loud in the background. Then she realised the song by The Crazy World of Arthur Brown was the message.

The music stopped abruptly on 'I'll see you *burn*'. Only someone with a warped sense of humour and a liking for retro music would leave her a message like that. She fully expected it to be followed by some sarcastic remark from MacRae that included the word *lady*. But no. There was a short pause then Sean's enthusiastic voice. 'Hi Rhona. Got here okay. It's great. You can reach me on this number . . .'

Rhona wrote down the number. Chance appeared at her feet winding in and out of her legs, looking for food. Rhona went back to the kitchen, fed the cat and raided the fridge for something for herself. It was then she noticed the set table. Place-mat, knife, fork and wine glass. A fresh red rose in a tumbler of water.

Fear trickled down her spine. The strange message

on the ansaphone. Now this. She stood very still, listening to the silent flat. Maybe it was Mrs Harper? That was a distinct possibility, one she could check easily enough. But the song on the ansaphone?

She walked through the flat, checking every room for signs of an intruder. All the windows were tight closed. Nothing was disturbed. Everything looked just as Sean would have left it.

14

DETECTIVE CONSTABLE JANICE Clarke had wordlessly warned Rhona on entry. DI Wilson was not a happy man. Janice was Bill's equivalent of Chrissy. They might have been related, not in looks but in attitude. Janice handed her two cups. The right-hand one was hot, the other cold, the milk already congealing. Just the way Bill liked it. The old leather chair creaked round.

'So, what's wrong with your face?' she asked.

'Long time since I heard that one.' Bill broke his sour expression with a half-smile. 'There's been a call from our friends in the East asking about the possibility of contaminated cocaine.'

'Thallium?'

'Maybe. They've had two serious cases of suspected drug contamination in the last two weeks. Both critically ill in hospital. And something else. There was a house fire early this morning on an Edinburgh council estate. They found the body of an addict inside.'

'I'll take a bet all three addicts lived in a run-down area earmarked for redevelopment,' Rhona said.

Bill nodded. 'All from the same estate.'

It was too much of a coincidence. 'Who's the developer?'

'A well-known and respected company, with interests all over Scotland,' Bill raised his eyebrows, 'including council redevelopment in Glasgow.'

'I take it you pointed that out to your Edinburgh equivalent?'

'The company has its headquarters in Edinburgh.'

'He reminded you of that?'

'And the fact that the chairman of the company is a pillar of Edinburgh society.'

'Surely you're not going to let that stop you.'

Bill gave her a look that suggested pigs might fly.

'Janice and I are working on it.'

'Could you get me details on firms manufacturing fireworks?' she asked.

'What for?'

'Thallium is used in green-emitting fireworks. And Edinburgh, as we both know, is big on fireworks.'

'Before you go . . .' Bill betrayed his concern. 'I think you should know a body's been found in the hills near Arrochar.'

Rhona took a seat, her legs suddenly weak. The horror of her last case – a paedophile ring that murdered vulnerable youths – had ended with the disappearance of the main suspect, a man who called himself Simon.

'Initial examination suggests it could be him. Dr Sissons is doing a post-mortem.' He paused. 'I can get someone else to do the forensic work if you want?'

'I'd rather do it myself.'

'We haven't tracked down all the members of the

ring. If he survived your attack and the fire at the cottage, he had contacts that would help him.'

'I know.'

'Let's hope it's him, then.'

She nodded. 'I'm going to drive through to Edinburgh.'

'Thought you might,' he smiled. 'Best of luck.'

The City of Edinburgh Council had tidied up the housing scheme twice in the past ten years. It had been a waste of time. The half-hearted makeover couldn't cover the rot inside. The soul had already departed.

Residents of the more salubrious parts of Edinburgh would have given their eye teeth for the hundreds of parking spaces that lined the grid of houses. An attempt had been made to install a heart when it was first built, with a block that held a cinema, a church, a couple of shops and a bookie's. The cinema had turned into a bingo hall, the shops shut except the post office and one determined butcher, who had obviously been made of strong stuff, repainting his graffiti-covered walls regularly. Rhona could make out the sedimentary layers of expletives under the thin white paint.

If MacFarlane was surprised to see her he didn't show it. When he emerged from the burned-out building, Rhona fully expected MacRae to follow him. She had steeled herself for it. But MacFarlane was alone.

'I take it the body's gone?' she asked.

'An hour ago.'

'I'll call in at Pathology.'

'Suit yourself. You know the Doc. Not too keen on the West poking its nose in our affairs.'

'We've had similar cases. It might help. Is MacRae involved with this one?' The words were out before she could stop them.

MacFarlane's face was impassive. 'Sev's taking some leave.'

So Gillian had got what she wanted.

'Want to take a look inside?'

At least MacFarlane took her seriously, she thought, then felt bad. MacRae had taken her seriously. They just sparked off each other like a tinder box and dry paper. Together they could have started a fire in a swimming pool.

There wasn't much left inside the council flat. In a corner lay half a dozen cans and what looked like the remains of bedding. There was an old-fashioned stuffed armchair and blackened bits of kitchen table. Rhona stepped round the charred remains.

'Where did you find the body?'

'Over there.'

MacFarlane pointed at the far wall. The SOCOs had drawn the body outline halfway up the wall, as if the victim had been propped against it. The wall was heavily smoke-marked and soaking wet from the deluge of water, but here and there lurid purple wallpaper was still visible.

'Did you find the remains of any pictures?' Rhona said.

'Pictures?'

'That might have fallen off the wall.'

MacFarlane shook his head uncomprehendingly.

'I just wondered what these were for.'

The nails were six-inchers. They stuck out rigidly from the wall, three feet apart.

'Did you see the victim's hands?' Rhona asked. She dropped her forensic bag beside her and flipped it open.

'Hands?' Obviously MacFarlane wasn't sharing her thoughts. 'The body was badly burned. That's all I know.'

Rhona pointed to the wall near the nails. 'Did your forensic team sample the wall here?'

'I don't know. I'd have to check.'

Rhona rubbed a filter paper round each nail then dropped on the reagents. She showed MacFarlane the pink result. By the look on his face, MacFarlane was catching up.

'I think he was crucified before the place was set on fire.'

MacFarlane hitched a lift back with her. She suspected he wanted to talk, or maybe make sure Dr MacKenzie would give her house-room at the post-mortem. MacFarlane's excuse was that he was short of squad cars and wanted to leave two for the constables doing the rounds asking questions of the residents.

'I don't like my men in there without a getaway vehicle,' he said.

He wasn't joking.

Rhona swung out onto the main road, which had been traffic-calmed with crazy paving and big ugly bollards. A few struggling trees survived inside their mesh cages. Yet the housing scheme's setting couldn't have been better. Easy access to the ring road, a shopping mall nearby, a short car journey through Holyrood Park to Scotland's parliament building and the city centre. Private housing was already encroaching from the east, neat semis, toy houses in red brick with pseudo-Georgian entrances.

MacFarlane took his time. They were nearly at the Pathology Lab before he asked her why she'd come back.

She told him about her conversation with Bill Wilson, the contaminated cocaine and the burn marks on the Glasgow boy's wrists.

'So we go one better, and nail ours to the wall?' he said grimly.

'Edinburgh always has to go one better. It's traditional.'

MacFarlane looked thoughtful. A spate of drug-related deaths linked by fire. But nothing to do with the city centre fires, which were potentially more disastrous. Rhona asked who was dealing with them.

'Sev's off and Gallagher's still in hospital. So it's down to me.'

'So why was I sent away?'

No answer.

She pulled over on a double yellow line.

'It was MacRae, wasn't it?'

MacFarlane hesitated. 'Sev thought you'd be safer in Glasgow.' He looked uncomfortable.

'I would never have left if I'd known.'

'That's why he did it.'

They were causing a traffic jam on the narrow road. She indicated and drew out.

'What happens now?'

'We continue our enquiries and hope we're wrong about the timing.'

'You'll let the Hogmanay party go ahead?'

'We have no choice.'

You couldn't cancel the biggest New Year party in the world on the strength of a unsubstantiated threat. She changed tack.

'What made MacRae think I was in danger?'

'There was a letter after the fire at his house. It mentioned your name.'

A fleeting picture entered Rhona's brain. A single red rose. A place-setting. The song on the ansaphone.

'You okay?' MacFarlane looked worried.

'Of course I'm okay,' she said shortly. 'What about Amy?'

'Gillian took her up north to her mother's for a while.'

'So what's MacRae doing with his leave?'

'Drinking.'

The Pathology Unit loomed up in front of them. Rhona drew into a reserved space and switched off.

The pathologist's voice had a war-weary tone. Heat contraction of the skin of a corpse often produced splits which might be interpreted as tears or cuts inflicted during life, he told her. The distinction between burns inflicted during life and burns inflicted on an already dead body could be difficult, if not impossible, to detect at autopsy.

'So you don't think he was nailed to the wall?' Bluntness seemed Rhona's only instrument.

MacKenzie's pale blue eyes rolled upwards as if she had just committed an Edinburgh social gaffe. 'I didn't say that.'

Rhona sought refuge in MacFarlane's encouraging look.

'Dr MacLeod took samples from around the nails we found in the wall,' he said. 'If this body wasn't nailed to the wall, then someone else was.'

The pathologist turned his blue stare on MacFarlane.

'The hands could have been injured prior to death.' The tone was grudging, but the words were enough.

'Do we know how he died?' Rhona asked.

'Come and have a look.'

MacKenzie waved them over to the body. Rhona followed, with MacFarlane a foot behind.

'The thoracic and abdominal walls are partly burned away, but the viscera are largely intact and show no evidence of natural disease.' MacKenzie pointed at a basin. 'Our victim's last meal. The usual healthy diet, pie beans and chips. Oh, and there was vomit in the oesophagus. The larynx, trachea and bronchi contained a large amount of soot and the lungs and major blood vessels were bright red.'

MacKenzie moved further down the body with Rhona following. MacFarlane stayed where he was.

'As you can see, the testes and external genitalia are burned away, but the presence of a prostate and seminal vesicles confirm the body is male.'

'Age?' Rhona said.

'The medial epiphyses of the clavicles were almost completely fused, so twenty-one or more. The lack of atheroma in the coronary arteries, aorta and other major vessels suggest he was certainly under forty. A young adult male.'

'Death by smoke inhalation?'

MacKenzie nodded. 'Most likely.'

So whatever torture he'd been through didn't mean he'd escaped the terror of the fire.

'Any clue as to his identity?' she asked.

'The body is too badly charred for visual recognition. However, there were some surviving items that might provide a clue.'

The pathologist left the table and brought over a small metal tray for inspection. The smell in the room was oppressive. Barbecues were swiftly losing their appeal.

'Would it be possible to establish the presence of thallium in the body?' Rhona asked.

The pathologist was simultaneously evaluating the possibility of meeting her request and the reason for it.

'In a similar case in Glasgow, there was some evidence to suggest the boy had been poisoned with thallium,' she enlarged.

'Really? God forbid that we should be following in Glasgow's footsteps.'

The pathologist took them into a side room to examine the contents of the tray and left them to it. When the door clicked shut behind him, MacFarlane's sigh of relief matched her own. Rhona laid the tray on the work surface and perched on the stool beside it. MacFarlane seemed to be intent on sucking in air from the air conditioner that whined above them.

'Last time we met it was me being sick,' she teased.

'And me taking the mickey.'

They exchanged smiles.

'Shall we take a look at the victim's prized possessions?'

Two small earrings and a key with a metal tag lay on the tray.

'Probably a front-door key,' she suggested.

'Not a Yale.' He picked it up and turned it over in his hand. 'There's something scratched on the tag.'

The clumsily-etched word looked like 'Robbie'.

MacFarlane climbed into the passenger seat.

'Any luck on the semen in the girl?' he asked as she drove away.

'It didn't match the letter,' she told him.

'And we have no way of knowing if it was rape or not.'

She shook her head. 'I want to see the letter with my name in it.'

MacFarlane looked uneasy.

'Forensic has it.'

MacFarlane had been planning a visit to Forensic, but not with her in tow. He was uncomfortable about her being there at all. Rhona tried to look on the bright side. Hopefully the threatening letter had reached Forensic without a sojourn in MacRae's stale glove compartment.

15

MACRAE HADN'T MOVED from the flat in the last twenty-four hours. Jaz glared at the first-floor window then took off for the corner café with the dog at his heels. It had been a waste of time giving MacRae the drawing and telling him about Mary. MacRae hadn't done a bloody thing since he'd seen him in the pub, except go on a bender. Jaz bit into the pie the waitress brought him and took a slurp of tea. He was losing income arsing about outside MacRae's flat, waiting for him to come out and get on with the job.

Jaz broke a piece of the pie and dropped it under the table along with a handful of chips. It was expensive feeding Emps. Karen must have spent most of her earnings on the dog.

He spent the rest of the morning selling the *Big Issue* and deciding what to do next. He could take his drawing and description to the police station. Ask to speak to MacFarlane. He didn't hold out much hope there. He would be lucky to get past the Desk Sergeant. As far as the police were concerned, he was a low-life and always would be.

A woman was approaching the café and for a moment he thought it was the forensic scientist. When she got nearer he realised he was wrong, but it gave him an idea. If MacRae wouldn't do anything, maybe she would. Jaz shoved the remaining magazines in his bag and set off along Princes Street towards the West End.

When Rhona called Greg at work, he told her there was no problem about staying at the flat again. He wouldn't be back that night, so she would have the place to herself. She planned to call Chrissy and bring her up to date but decided not to mention the threatening letter that MacFarlane had allowed her to photocopy, against his better judgement.

At Greg's, she poured herself a glass of wine and ran a bath. She would have to seek out MacRae and persuade him to come back on the case, she decided. MacFarlane had been loyal enough not to confess how worried he was. MacRae might be the only hope of outmanoeuvring the arsonist before he struck again. Lying in the bath, Rhona reread the photocopied letter.

The contents showed a strong link between fire and sexual excitement. The author also hated women. Karen's genitalia had been burned before the fire started. The arsonist had moved on. Setting a building alight was no longer enough.

This was why MacRae hadn't wanted her around, she thought. Why he'd tried to get rid of her at their first meeting. Why he'd got MacFarlane to recall her to Glasgow.

She examined the text of the letter again. The words were all lower case except for an occasional capital letter. She wrote the letters in a sequence along the bottom of the page. They didn't make a word, but they did look familiar.

After she'd dried and dressed, she pulled out her laptop and opened the anonymous email. The letters were in a different order, but they were the same. I C H B U N R T E B T H. The more she stared at the characters, the more she realised it couldn't be a coincidence. She began by isolating the three vowels. She would assume there were at least two words, maybe three, each with a vowel. She made up 'burn', then concentrated on the other letters. Once she separated the word 'the', it was easy. BURN THE BITCH. The person sending the emails was the person writing the letters.

The sharpness of the buzzer interrupted her. The male voice on the intercom was a mixture of belligerence and apology. 'I have to talk to you about Mac-Rae.'

'You'd better come up.'

He stood in the hall taking in the polished French tiles, the glistening glass chandelier, the deep rug. Rhona wanted to tell him she felt the same when she saw Greg's flat for the first time, that her flat was a mess of cat hair and forensic journals. Instead she pointed the way through to the even more palatial sitting room.

The jacket that passed her was damp across the shoulders and the dark ponytail glistened with rain.

'Can I get you a coffee? Warm you up?'

She thought he was about to refuse then he relaxed and nodded, rubbing his hands together in front of the fire.

'Yeah. That would be great.'

When she came back from putting the kettle on, he was sitting on the couch with the dog sprawled at his feet.

'Some place.'

She smiled. 'Yes, but unfortunately not mine.'

'Oh.' He looked perturbed. 'I thought . . .'

'I live in Glasgow,' she explained. 'This is a friend's flat. He lets me stay when I come through.'

'Good friend.'

'Yes, he is.'

Rhona went back to the kitchen to make the coffee. Through the open door she observed his profile, almost feminine with the ponytail hanging over his shoulder. Rhona wondered if she had been wise to let him in, especially when Greg wasn't here. There were a lot of things lying about the place, things that could be slipped into his pocket, sold later for drugs or drink. Rhona chided herself as she poured the coffee. Just because Jaz was homeless didn't make him a criminal.

She brought through the coffee.

'The night after we talked about Karen, were you hanging about outside?'

Belligerence was back in his reply. 'I've been watching you and MacRae. I gave him a copy of this.'

He handed her a drawing. She examined it.

'This is very good.'

'I used to be an art student.' His voice was bitter. 'Before I screwed up.'

Rhona wanted to ask him what had gone wrong with his life, how he had ended up on the street. Instead she asked why the person in the drawing was important.

'I think he's Karen's murderer.'

'Why didn't you take the drawing to the police?'

His face darkened. 'Yeah, right.' He took the picture from her, stuffed it in his pocket and stood up.

'Thanks for the coffee.'

'Where are you going?'

'Not to the fuckin' police anyway.'

Rhona caught his arm. 'Don't leave yet. I'm sorry . . . I don't know your name?'

'Jaz,' he said relenting. 'My friends call me Jaz.'

'Well Jaz. I think it's time we talked properly, don't you?'

When Jaz left, Rhona went through to Greg's office, faxed the drawing to Chrissy and asked her to look through all the fire video footage they had. Some fire-raisers liked to watch the results of their exploits, so maybe there was a face in a crowd that fitted. She would check the Edinburgh footage herself.

Rhona sat down, suddenly tired. She knew she was only skirting the problem. At least when she had biological materials to work on she felt she was doing something constructive. The only person who seemed to have a handle on the arsonist was MacRae. And it seemed he had given up. She called DI MacFarlane and asked him for MacRae's address. He was silent for a moment. 'You're wasting your time. He's already made up his mind.'

'Then I'll have to change it for him.'

16

LOTHIAN ROAD WAS choked with traffic until she got beyond Tollcross. MacFarlane had given her directions to MacRae's flat. Take a right at Tollcross and head up the hill past Bruntsfield Links. Viewforth was somewhere on the right. She missed the turning and had to pull in and ask a *Big Issue* seller stationed outside the Royal Bank of Scotland. He pointed her back the way she'd come.

'Second on the left,' he informed her cheerily.

She bought a magazine in thanks.

MacRae's flat was on the top floor of the block. She pressed the buzzer and waited. She was about to press again when he answered gruffly.

'Yeah?'

'It's Rhona MacLeod. Can I come up?'

There was a heavy silence, then the stair door opened. He was waiting at the door, towel round his neck, hair wet. Behind him the room emitted a smell of alcohol and shower gel.

'Sorry,' she said.

He looked her up and down. 'About what? My body?'

'I thought we'd got past that stage,' she shot back at him.

'What stage?'

'The women-are-for-laying stage.'

'Never. Call me old-fashioned if you like.' He threw the towel to some hidden spot behind the door and waited, hands on hips.

'Can I come in?'

He stood back to let her past. 'Be my guest.'

He closed the door behind her.

'So, Dr Rhona MacLeod. What is it you want?'

'MacFarlane said you refused to help.'

'MacFarlane is right,' he said quietly.

The thought crossed Rhona's mind that she could walk away from this man, report her findings to Bill Wilson, take a few days off, visit Sean in Amsterdam. The scenario was an attractive one.

'We can help,' she said, determined.

His voice was low and angry. 'Take my advice, lady. Go back to Glasgow.' He reached for a T-shirt from the back of a chair.

'You never listen to anyone, do you?' she flung at him. 'No wonder your wife left you.'

He turned, his face furious.

'What did you say?'

Saying it once was stupid. Repeating it would be insane.

'I said, no wonder your wife left you.'

A nerve played the corner of his mouth. The scarring that crept over his shoulders looked blue. He was so close she could smell him. Soap and anger.

'For your information, Gillian left me because of this.'

He pointed to the scars.

'She didn't like to see it, or feel it. It reminded her of what I do.'

There was naked hurt in his eyes.

'Sean doesn't like what I do either.'

MacRae shrugged. 'Then we're two of a kind.'

'Except I don't give up.'

'You don't have a child.'

Rhona opened her mouth to tell him she did have a child, that she had tasted the same fear. Instead she said: 'MacFarlane said Gillian took Amy north.'

'As far away from me as possible.' He smiled grimly.

'Then she's safe.'

He turned away, dismissing her. 'I've told MacFarlane all I know.'

'Jaz gave you important information and you did nothing about it.'

He reached for a half-empty bottle of whisky and tipped some into a glass.

'I was busy.' He threw back the whisky.

'Then I'll have to deal with it alone.'

'Don't let me keep you.'

His door shut as she reached the bottom of the stairs. All the way down, she'd hoped he would call her back.

17

THE STREET WAS narrow, dipping down steeply and curving beneath the thoroughfare above. Edinburgh had a multitude of streets like this. Roads under roads. Layers of houses whose basements sat lightly on the past. Dig in your basement in the Old Town and you were likely to find a cobbled street, or the remnants of a medieval sewer. Ghost tour companies thrived on the warren of pathways and hovels that lurked beneath their more modern counterparts.

Rhona reached the address on the drawing and parked outside on a double yellow line. MacFarlane should be there within ten minutes. After waiting twenty minutes she locked the car, ran through the rain and ducked into the low entrance-way, hoping the squat door would be open. She was in luck. Someone had wedged it tight against the frame with a piece of wood, but it wasn't hard to free it and push her way in.

The building was in semi-darkness, the air musty. Rhona ran her hand along the wall, searching for a light switch. It gave a reassuring click but nothing happened. Whatever Mary Queen of Scots was using for light, it wasn't electricity. In front of her, a set of steps were splashed with green light from an overhead grating. She counted six before they twisted out of sight.

She had reached the bottom of the stairs when she heard the muffled sound of footsteps above her.

Instinct told her it wasn't MacFarlane.

The green light was cut off as a figure began its descent. Rhona pressed herself behind the curve of the staircase. Whoever was coming down would sense her soon, if he hadn't already. This room was larger than the one upstairs, although lower in height. There was nowhere to hide.

When he lunged at her Rhona was ready. Already lower than him, she brought her knee up as hard as she could, catching him full between the legs. He doubled up, swearing obscenely. Rhona launched herself upwards but a hand gripped her ankle, bringing her down heavily on the stone steps. Now it was her turn to swear.

'Rhona?' MacRae was lying on his side, knees to chin, his face as green as the stairwell light.

'What the hell are you doing here?'

'You asked me here, remember?' he choked.

'I didn't ask you to attack me.'

'Why didn't you call out?' He was dragging himself onto his knees, his expression curdling from agony to anger.

'Why didn't you?' she threw back.

'Christ, woman!'

'Don't "Christ, woman" me! I was here doing the job you refused to do, remember?'

'Move over,' he groaned, pulling himself onto the

step beside her, cradling his crotch. 'I've heard of ball breakers, but you take the prize.'

She caught his eye and started to laugh.

'No,' he pleaded painfully.

She waited while he regained his composure.

'What do we do now?'

'We wait for MacFarlane,' he said.

Without torches a search in the squat was useless. They had abandoned the attempt and were now sitting in the Saab. MacRae reached over and opened the glove compartment.

'You're not looking for a drink?'

'Too right I am.' MacRae extracted a can of Irn-Bru, opened it and drank it in a oner.

'What did you think of the letters?' he said.

'I'm pretty sure four are from the same person. I'm not a handwriting expert, but the tone and style are the same, plus the sexual innuendo. Your report to Mac-Farlane said the last four major fires have been deliberately started, probably by the same man?'

MacRae stared out of the window. There was no rain now, just a biting cold wind that seeped through the joints of the old Saab.

He nodded. 'A letter for every major fire.'

'Plus the warning to MacFarlane suggesting the next fire will be tonight,' Rhona paused, 'and the latest letter threatening you . . . and me.'

'MacFarlane showed you that?'

She nodded.

'Well I hope you like shit, because it looks like we're in it.'

'Deeper than you think.' Rhona handed him the photocopy. 'The capital letters make up the phrase at the bottom.'

'So what?' he shrugged. 'This is a nutcase. He likes to hide insults inside his other insults.'

'He likes to email them too.'

His careless tone had gone. 'The wanker's been emailing you?'

''I've had three anonymous emails, sent to the lab. They were just a string of jumbled capital letters. These letters.'

'And?'

'I didn't try to work out what they said . . . until this.'

'Is there anyone who might have it in for you?'

'I've testified in court lots of times. My evidence often helps the prosecution case.'

'But anything to do with fire?' he insisted.

Rhona shook her head. 'Sex crimes, murder . . .'

MacRae had slipped into thought. 'These emails . . . they started before you came to work with me?' They must have started about the same time as the Glasgow fires. She told him so.

MacRae looked puzzled. 'The city centre fires are different from the house fires,' he said. 'The house fires were lit to cover up something.'

'What?'

'You're the forensic expert.'

'The pathologist thought the dead girl in the Princes Street fire might have been raped.

'That doesn't fit.' MacRae shook his head. 'Fire's the sexual turn-on.'

'So?'

'The girl was in the wrong place at the wrong time. Somebody got to her first. If she was raped, you've got two crimes to solve.'

'Thanks very much.'

'Me, I'm only interested in this one.'

'We had no luck matching the DNA profile from the letter to the database.'

'The world and his brother know about DNA. When he sent that letter he was effectively saying, Fuck you! He knew we would try to match him and he knew we couldn't because he has no record.'

They had nothing on him. Nothing but his threats.

'Who is he?' she said.

MacRae was silent for a moment. 'He's fascinated by fire to the point that he shuts out everything else. It's a powerful act of creation. He wants it to go on growing. We kill it. So next time he has to make it bigger and more powerful. One we can't destroy.'

Silence settled over them. Outside, the wind moaned.

'How did you burn your back?'

MacRae didn't look surprised by her change of tack, as if he'd been expecting the question.

'I was seventeen. There was a deserted warehouse where me and my mates hung out. We would light a fire and sit round talking. Then one night I got lucky. This girl came with us. She and I left the fire and went into the shadows. That was when the explosion came. My pal Mikey was killed, his face blown away. The other two boys were badly burned. The girl was shielded by me.'

'What caused the explosion?'

'We had built our fire over an old chemical tank. The concrete floor expanded and had nowhere to go. It shattered, throwing lumps round us. The tank underneath was cracked. Whoosh!' He made a face. 'The most memorable sex I ever had.' He smiled cynically. 'So you see, he could be me.'

'MacFarlane was right. You do know him.'

'Not well enough.'

She was silent for a moment.

'Maybe we're wrong. Maybe the fires were lit for other reasons. Fraud, insurance? Maybe the letters are just a wind-up.'

'MacFarlane's found no evidence of fraud. We've had a letter for every fire,' he said. 'Either the letter-writer's lighting the fires, or he knows who is.'

'I wonder . . .' she said.

'What?'

'This person knows fire like you,' she hesitated. 'Could he be a fireman?'

'We've checked out all current personnel.'

'Okay. What about someone who used to be in the Brigade? Someone with a grudge against you.'

He shook his head.

'A long shot, but I'll think about it.'

They lapsed into silence until MacFarlane arrived five minutes later and they joined him in Queen Mary's *pied à terre*. MacFarlane gasped on his first deep breath inside the door. 'I hope the hospital authorities gave the Queen a bath. It smells like shit in here.'

He shouted for a light and a constable arrived with three heavy-duty torches. The trio of beams swept the desolate scene.

'Get your men to look for anything inflammable. Petrol cans, anything like that.' MacRae nodded at Rhona. 'Come on.'

At the bottom of the steps, torchlight revealed the room they had fought in, followed by a long, unevenly floored passageway with openings on either side.

Rhona sniffed. 'Can you smell methane?'

MacRae turned his torch on the roof. 'We must be near the main sewer. It runs the length of Princes Street.'

'Would that give someone access to all the buildings?'

'No, but it has benching either side, so you can walk through it. The Brigade uses it for training in sewer rescues. Pipes go up the buildings and vent onto their roofs to avoid a build-up of methane down here. Dangerous stuff.'

Rhona didn't need reminding. Methane's smell wasn't its only undesirable quality. Rhona was struggling to make sense of Jaz's suspicions. 'Why would the guy who attacked Mary want access to here?'

'Who said he did? Maybe he set Mary's hair alight because she smelt bad. We have no proof that he has anything to do with the fires at all.'

'But he wanted her out of the building. Jaz said so.'

'Jaz told us what Mary told him. Mary's an alkie.

Hallucination is her middle name. She thinks she's Mary Queen of Scots, for God's sake!' MacRae ended irritably.

What MacRae said was true. There was nothing down here but a bad smell.

Rhona left MacRae running his torch round the walls of the room while she headed down the narrow passage, flashing her torch into each opening. The floor was treacherously uneven. She caught her toe on a jagged edge of stone and only broke her fall by grabbing at the wall. Despite the light from the torch, her progress was slow. The rooms on either side varied in size. Some were little more than a hole in the wall, some opened onto larger areas. All were empty.

'Rhona?'

'Down here.'

MacRae's shadow advanced before him, thick and black. Rhona felt grateful for his presence.

'How far to the end?' he called in exasperation.

'About five yards. Then it peters out in a brick wall. Probably the foundations of a building.'

'So there's nothing?' MacRae was as disappointed as she was. His torch swept round the corner and onto her face.

'Watch it!' Rhona shouted, knowing it was too late. MacRae's strides were at least one-and-a-half hers. She had missed the hole, just off-centre in the passage-way. MacRae didn't. He cursed as the torch hit the floor and went out.

'Thanks for the warning!'

'Are you okay?'

'Apart from the broken leg, you mean?'

'It can't be that bad.'

'How the hell would you know?' He removed his leg from the hole and stuck his head down instead. 'Hold on,' he said, 'I've found the source of the smell.'

When MacFarlane appeared minutes later he found them both on their knees.

'This hole opens into the main sewer,' MacRae informed him. 'Somebody's taken off the cover. Look, there it is against the wall. MacFarlane, check with Scottish Water. See if anyone's been down here recently.'

MacFarlane nodded. 'Where are you going?'

MacRae was already poised over the hole.

'To take a look.'

'Let's get a Scottish Water engineer down here first.' MacFarlane looked worried.

MacRae ignored him and handed Rhona his torch.

'I'll give you a shout when I'm down.'

He dropped through the hole.

Rhona held the torch above the hole hoping he could make it out in the darkness, then dropped it.

'I'm going to walk along a bit,' he shouted up. 'I won't be long.'

MacFarlane tried his mobile. 'I'll have to go up. I can't get a signal here.' Rhona waited until he was out of sight then climbed down the manhole after MacRae.

Fifteen metal rungs down, and her feet were on solid ground. To her right, dark water flowed through a brick tunnel. They should have waited for breathing apparatus, but she, like MacRae, was too impatient. She breathed in. Her throat was clear, her eyes didn't sting. There was methane, but at a manageable level.

MacRae's footsteps suggested he had gone to the left. Rhona swung her torch and headed in the opposite direction.

Not far along, another channel met the main sewer. She started to follow it. The roof here was lower and she had to keep her head well down, sweeping her torch in a wide arc in front of her, trying to ignore the excited squeaks of disturbed rats. Ten yards further, just as she was on the point of turning back, she spotted a series of long, thin blue lines on the curved brick wall.

Rhona dropped to her knees for a closer look.

Rhona reached up and caught MacRae's helping hand out of the manhole. MacFarlane was back. He looked relieved as she emerged. 'You shouldn't have gone down there without breathing apparatus,' Sev told her, for the benefit of MacFarlane.

'You did.'

He shrugged. 'Find anything interesting?'

'Something was dragged along one of the side sewers that run down to the Nor Loch,' she told him. 'I found fresh paint scrapings on the wall.'

MacRae looked thoughtful.

'Scottish Water don't know about this opening. It's not on their plan,'

MacFarlane said. 'I think we should find out what's been dragged along there,'

Rhona insisted. MacFarlane looked puzzled.

'What's so special about a scrape of paint?' Rhona looked at MacRae to see if he was thinking the same as her. He was.

'It's not the paint,' she told MacFarlane. 'It's where it came from.'

18

THE TRAIN WASN'T busy. Jaz would normally have hidden in the toilet and saved himself the fare, but with all the terrorist threats you had to have a ticket. It felt good to travel legally. He could sit and watch the countryside go by instead of keeping an eye out for an inspector.

Funding the train fare wasn't his only problem. He would have to work overtime next week to pay the rent. Finding Karen's killer was proving expensive, what with feeding Emps and the time he was spending off the job. But he didn't care. Karen should never have died.

Scotland threw itself past the window in a flurry of rain and the odd beautiful moment when the clouds parted and the sun shone through. They had passed the Highland boundary fault line and the hills rose, steeply wooded, on either side of the track.

Going north had been a split-second decision. He'd seen MacRae saying goodbye to his wife and kid in the station and jumped the train. He'd been thinking of bailing out of Edinburgh for a while anyway. Poking his nose into the attack on Mary had brought him too much interest from some quarters.

Jaz pressed his face to the glass. The warmer air in the compartment had steamed up the window. He wiped a patch and stared through, following the skyline. Mist hung in tendrils among the sharp pine trees. Jaz found himself remembering some of his favourite landscape paintings, the images that had set him on course to Art College in the first place. Soon, he promised himself, he would paint again.

He'd got on the train two carriages back from MacRae's wife and kid, then walked through. As he passed them the wee girl had reached out to pat the dog, but her mother pulled her back, telling her sharply that not all dogs were friendly.

'Your mum's right,' Jaz said. 'But this one is. Look.' He made Emps offer a paw and the girl had shaken it in delight. MacRae's wife had softened then and let her stroke the big head.

'My gran's got a dog called Bess,' she confided in him. 'We're going to see her.'

'That's nice,' he smiled back.

He'd considered sitting down next to them then thought better of it.

'I'd better keep going,' he said. 'Say goodbye, Emps.'

'Emps. That's a good name.'

He told her it was short for Emperor, then with an attempt at a smile at her mother he moved on.

Settled in the next carriage, he went over the other occupants of the train in his head. Most of the voices were Scottish although he'd spotted an American couple near the back of his carriage. There was no one suspicious-looking. No one except himself.

When he spotted Mrs MacRae gathering her luggage, Jaz got up and headed for the door. The American couple were already there, bags piled up in front of them.

Jaz accepted their offer of a ride to the village, in the hope that both the car that picked Amy up and the taxi would head in the same direction. They did. He was only minutes into a conversation about the beauties of Scotland, rain and all, when the car in front took a left turn. Jaz asked his hosts to let him off fifty yards further along.

'But there's nothing here,' the woman said looking round.

Jaz gestured in the direction of a distant barn.

'I can take a shortcut across the fields,' he explained. 'Give Emperor some exercise.'

It had been too easy finding them, Jaz told himself as he eased into position in the wet undergrowth within sight of the cottage. If he could find them, anyone could.

MacRae's wife appeared at the door of the cottage an hour later followed by another woman, obviously her mother. They had a short conversation which Jaz strained to catch. Whatever they were saying they didn't want the wee girl to hear. Then the two of them headed for the car parked in the drive and Jaz caught their final exchange.

'You'll have to go back some time, you know.'

MacRae's wife didn't look convinced.

'You can't keep them apart. Whatever Sev is, he loves his daughter.'

'I'm aware of that,' came the sharp reply. 'Can we change the subject?'

'I'll be back by teatime. You'll be alright here on your own?'

The response was short and tinged with suppressed fear.

'Of course.'

The old woman patted her daughter's arm. 'Keep Bess in the garden if Amy's out. She'll look after her.'

MacRae's wife tried a laugh. 'You're beginning to sound as paranoid as me,' she said.

Jaz shifted himself, easing the cramp in his right calf. The sodden shoulders of his parka were clamped to his skin like a neck brace. The rain was off for the moment and sunshine tentatively broke the pattern of grey. If Emps had been here he wouldn't have been so cold. Karen was right. Emps kept you warm.

The door opened and the wee girl came running out onto the grass. Behind her padded a big golden labrador. Jaz was glad he'd had the sense to leave Emps in the barn. All he needed was two dogs sniffing one another out.

The labrador paced the lawn. If it caught his scent, it made no move to come towards him, choosing instead to stay close to the girl. She was scuffling around under a big pine tree, at last securing what she was looking for. She threw the stick and it whizzed towards Jaz, landing three feet in front of his hiding place. He held his breath and lay perfectly still, planning what he would say when the dog discovered him.

The rheumy eyes found the stick and the greying muzzle sniffed at it. After what seemed a lifetime the dog lifted the stick and headed back. Jaz hoped that would be the end of it, but no. The stick came whizzing back. It flew over the fence to his left. Bess was making a valiant effort this time, running as fast as her fat stomach would allow. She stuck her nose through the fence and whined at the irretrievable stick.

'Bess!'

The white socks with the pink trim were on their way. He would give her another metre then stand up. Better to pretend he was looking for his dog than be caught lying in the undergrowth.

'Amy! Where are you?'

The socks stopped. The child reached down. Jaz caught a glimpse of dark hair as she selected a different stick. He could have sworn their eyes met, then she was up.

'I'm coming.'

'I told you not to leave the garden.'

Amy was indignant. 'I didn't leave the garden. I threw the stick as far as the fence. Bess couldn't find it. I had to get another one.'

The woman made an effort to sound normal.

'Granny'll be home soon. Come in and help me set the table for tea.'

Jaz watched as the door shut behind them.

Darkness was gathering. From the kitchen window, his shadow would be one of many. Jaz eased himself up and stood for a minute, letting the blood run into his cramped limbs. The smell of wood smoke from the cottage was making him think of food. He ignored the empty feeling in his stomach and tried to work out what to do.

The occupants of the cottage weren't planning on going anywhere tonight. He could take a chance and go and get Emps from the barn.

The barn was silent as he approached but as soon as he drew close he heard a low growl, which soon transformed into a welcoming whine. When he opened the barn door, Emps nearly knocked him over in his delight.

Inside it was warm and dry. Bales of hay, stacked at the back, emitted the smell of summer. Emps pranced about, pieces of straw flying from his coat.

'Good sleep, eh Emps?'

The dog licked his hand. It would be hard to leave the barn, but he had no choice. He'd already decided on their resting place for the night. The garage at the cottage might not have the warmth of the barn, but it would do.

Emperor bounded out the door ahead of him.

'Wait, Emps.'

There was a yelp, then silence. Jaz ran outside. The dog was nowhere to be seen.

'Emps! Come here, boy.'

There was a sudden movement behind him. Jaz swung round just as something hard and heavy

smashed down on his head. He groaned, pain screaming through him.

The second blow hit him. With a soft grunt, Jaz
slipped to the ground, unconscious.

19

THEY HAD ADJOURNED to MacRae's office. Rhona was surprised by its relative cleanliness, then remembered he had spent the last twenty-four hours holed up at home.

'With a bit of luck the rain will keep the punters away tonight,' MacRae suggested hopefully.

MacFarlane shook his head. 'The Met says to expect a clear night for the *Night Afore Fiesta*.'

'Just our luck.'

The sewer plan was spread on the desk; detailed entrances and underground walkways for sewer maintenance, a city beneath a city.

''We need to get a list of all those who have access to this information,' Rhona suggested.

MacFarlane nodded. 'We're doing that.'

Rhona looked at them both. 'It's a lot of time and man hours for a vague threat and a gut feeling.'

'The message from above is to take reasonable precautions. Nothing else.' MacFarlane looked apologetic.

Rhona could imagine the City Fathers' response. Edinburgh was set to make a lot of money from the next few days. The last thing they would want was the threat of arson keeping the crowds away. She felt sorry for MacFarlane. A hunch wasn't currency in this regime of balance sheets.

'The traffic stops at 5.30,' MacFarlane went on. 'We can do a full security check of the street before we let the crowds in.'

'And the sewer?' Rhona asked.

'Scottish Water's responsibility.'

'It would be difficult for an arsonist to get something set up while the shops are still trading,' MacRae said.

'Unless he has access to a basement,' Rhona reminded him.

MacFarlane was looking more worried by the minute. Clearing and searching Princes Street would be a major exercise, requiring time and manpower, neither of which he had. It would also attract interest. He voiced what they were all thinking.

'Maybe you were right.' He looked at MacRae. 'Maybe he wants us to concentrate on the Hogmanay celebrations while he goes elsewhere.'

MacRae looked grim. 'Well, we're about to find out.'

Rhona pressed the lab number. She would have to get back to Glasgow soon. It didn't take the numerous messages on her voice-mail from Chrissy to remind her where her real job was. Besides, officially Edinburgh didn't want her services. Bill Wilson had made that clear. She was here by her own choice.

'Dr MacLeod. I thought you were dead.'

'Thanks very much.'

'In fact, we were about to appoint a new Head of Department,' Chrissy went on.

'I get the point.'

'No you don't.' Chrissy's voice was serious. 'There's a murder case here you're supposed to be working on.'

'They've decided it was murder?'

'There were sufficient traces of thallium in the victim's body to cause death.'

'I take it you're to be the new Head of Department?' Rhona said laughing.

'Of course. Seriously though, when are you coming back?'

'Tomorrow,' Rhona said. 'Whatever happens.'

'Sounds ominous.'

'Tell Bill I asked Dr MacKenzie to look for thallium in the latest Edinburgh body. Find out if any traces were found.'

She rang off, promising to be back as soon as possible. Chrissy replied with a cynical 'Yeah'.

Neither man looked round when Rhona re-entered the room. 'There's nothing down there, Sev,' MacFarlane was saying. 'You checked the sewer yourself.'

'If you're going back down I want to go with you,' Rhona interrupted MacRae's glare.

'There's no need,' MacFarlane was firm. 'Scottish Water are checking.' He concentrated on MacRae. 'Go home for a while. Phone your kid.'

MacRae glanced at Rhona.

She pulled a face. 'We could both do with a shower.'

'Okay.' He seemed resigned. 'I'll see you back here in an hour.'

The call came through on MacFarlane's mobile as

she was about to leave. Rhona watched MacFarlane's face register puzzlement then concern. He waved her back from the door.

'That was Chemistry. They think the paint flakes were . . .'

She interrupted him. 'From a canister.'

His face was drawn. 'Of the type normally used for propane.'

Rhona tried to sound positive. 'Maybe it belonged to Scottish Water.'

MacFarlane wanted to believe her. 'I'll check.'

'Assuming nothing happens tonight, I'll have to show face in Glasgow tomorrow,' she told him.

'I understand.'

Traffic was thick round the sealed-off city centre. It took Rhona twenty minutes to get to Greg's flat. It was empty, although there were signs that Greg had come and gone. He'd opened a bottle of red wine and drunk half of it with a quick meal. Rhona had no qualms about pouring a glass to take into the shower.

She stripped off and dropped her clothes in a heap in the corner, stepped under the cascading water and began going over the list of events in her head.

Thallium poisoning in the Glasgow victim coupled with the fact that he had been tortured suggested a drugs war of some kind. If she was right and the Edinburgh victim had been crucified and then set alight, they only needed thallium to be detected in his system to link the two deaths. Neither death could yet be linked to the torched commercial property in Edinburgh, but instinct told her they were. She just didn't know how . . . yet. As for the threats to herself and MacRae . . .

Rhona turned off the shower and stepped out, the jigsaw incomplete.

When the front door opened she thought it was Greg coming back. She called 'Hi' from the kitchen and finished stuffing the dirty clothes into the washer-dryer. When she emerged, someone else stood in the hall.

20

JAZ OPENED HIS eyes. His head was throbbing so hard he couldn't think and his hands were pinioned at a 90 degree angle to the wall. The wire wound round his wrists was threatening to slice through his flesh like a cheese cutter. Jaz adjusted his stance in a vain effort to take the weight off his arms and tried to remember what had happened.

They'd been leaving the barn. He'd heard Emps yelp and he'd run outside, but the dog wasn't there. Then some bastard had hit him over the head.

He caught the smell of cigarette smoke as a figure emerged from the shadows; a man with hair cropped to the skull.

'Tommy!'

'Long time no see.'

Jaz couldn't believe his eyes. He hadn't seen Tommy since prison.

'What the fuck are you doing here?' Jaz said.

'Could say the same to you.' Tommy came closer as if to inspect his handiwork.

'Gonnae untie me, Tommy?' Tommy wasn't re-nowned for having a soft heart but it was worth a try. 'My shoulders are killing me.'

Tommy's smile would have curdled milk.

'Can't do that, mate. Not before you tell me what you're doing here. Orders, you know.'

Tommy Moffat had been thrown out of the army for not obeying orders. Doing what someone else told him was anathema to him. Jaz had spent two years with people like Tommy. It frightened him now to remember it. Even when his own brain was scrambled, the way Tommy treated folk had scared the hell out of him.

'You've been pissing off a few folk, Jaz.'

Tommy was sauntering round him, wearing the same vicious, sardonic look Jaz remembered only too well.

'Look, Tommy . . .'

'I heard you were working your passage back to Art College.'

'I am.'

Tommy was pulling something from his hip pocket. Jaz instinctively pressed himself against the wall but it wasn't a knife that emerged. It was a hammer.

'That's a pity,' Tommy fished in the other pocket. 'I havnae heard of a painter with nae hands.'

Jaz didn't have time to scream. The three-inch nail was through his right hand and into the barn wall with one hard blow. The second blow brought vomit to his mouth. Tommy lightly sidestepped the projectile.

'Now, a man with one good hand might still be able to paint.' Tommy kicked some straw over the offending mess. 'So, Jaz, want to keep one good hand?'

Jaz would have raised his head if he could. As it was

all his strength was in his body, lifting its weight off his arm and the crucified hand.

Tommy was selecting another nail. 'Now's the time to tell me why you're here, Jazzy boy.' He sighed. 'Otherwise it's byesy-bye to your painting career.'

'Jesus, Tommy.' The words escaped in a hiss of pain. 'Give us a chance.'

Tommy was looking at him, head on one side, enjoying himself.

'I'll tell you, right?'

He dragged a bale of hay nearer to Jaz.

'A wee warning, pal,' he said as he made himself comfortable. 'Make it good. I'm not here to listen to Jackanory.'

Jaz twisted his head round to look at his one good hand. Tommy was getting careless. Concentrating too much on his sadistic pleasures. The wire was looser now. Jaz worked on the wrist, turning it backwards and forwards. Every turn brought a stab of fire to his other hand. A dozen twists and his hand slid out. Letting his arm fall to his side was almost worse than holding it at ninety degrees to his body. Jaz buried his mouth in the collar of his parka. Now he had to pull the nail out.

Jaz sank to the ground and curled in a ball, the damaged hand clutched to his chest. After a few minutes he realised he was moaning Mammy, Mammy, Mammy. It struck him as weird since his Mammy had never been there when he needed her. After a while the pain was bearable and he could stand up. He dropped the parka on the floor and pulled off his top. It was clean at least. He wrapped his bad hand in it and pulled the parka back on.

By rights he should go, hit the road, jump on the train and disappear until things had cooled. But he wasn't going to. Jaz had never thought of himself as brave. Sticking a needle in his arm was as brave as he had ever got. And Robbie. Jaz tried not to play back the scene in his head that Tommy had described so vividly. Robbie had got in the way and Tommy had removed him. Jaz was getting in the way and Tommy was warning him. Jaz was the lucky one, but to convince Tommy he wasn't up north to spy on him, he'd had to say something about Amy.

The moon was a sliver of cream in a starred sky. Jaz tucked his bleeding hand under his left arm and headed for the cottage.

The wind felt like ice against his face. He used his teeth and his good hand to pull in the cord at the neck of the parka. He circled the garden. If Tommy jumped him now, he wouldn't stand a chance. A hammer wasn't Tommy's usual weapon. He usually preferred to pierce with something other than a nail.

The cottage sat in silence, the curtains drawn. Now he was here, Jaz had no idea what to do. If only Emps was with him. Tears sprung to his eyes. He didn't want to think what might have happened to the dog.

He made for the garage. Keeping low crossing the back garden, eyes on the light from the windows, he literally fell over the dog's dead body.

Bess lay on her side, eyes open, teeth bared in a

death-like grimace. Her head was pulled up and back, the red mark of Tommy's handiwork dividing her neck in two. Jaz slumped beside the warm body, knowing Tommy must have been here only minutes before. Then he noticed that the back door of the cottage stood open, light spilling out onto the grass.

21

'WHERE THE FUCK is she?'

'We talked about the paint then she left,' MacFarlane shouted back. 'She said she'd be here in an hour.'

Sev knew shouting at MacFarlane wasn't going to produce Rhona, but it made him feel better.

'Have you tried the friend's flat? Her mobile?'

'Yes and yes. The mobile's switched to the answering service.' MacFarlane shrugged his shoulders. 'Give her time. If she's having something to eat . . .'

Sev forced his attention back to the plan. 'She thinks there might be propane down there?'

'But where?' MacFarlane said. 'We've searched the length of the sewer. How could we miss gas canisters?'

'The channels that link the Princes Street sewer with the Nor Loch sewer, have they all been checked?'

'We can't check every drain in a couple of hours.' MacFarlane's voice was weary.

'This one meets the Princes Street sewer near where Rhona found the paint samples,' Sev stabbed at the paper, 'I'm going to take a look.' For once MacFarlane didn't argue.

The number of people swarming around the city

centre made Sev nervous. There were too many chil-
dren. How can you arrange a family event, MacFarlane had said, then tell them not to bring the kids?

Sev looked up at the sky. Clear as a bell with a wee
thin moon. The Scottish weather had perversely
decided to go dry.

There were police about, some in uniform, some
not. MacFarlane had got an agreement to up the police
presence. That was all. If there had been a bomb alert,
they would have taken notice.

Sev headed for Mary's former squat. The punk with
the dog had been right about that connection. Come to
think of it, he hadn't seen Jaz since their meeting in the
pub. He made up his mind to ask MacFarlane if he was
still hanging around.

Mary Queen of Scots' palace had been cleared but it
still smelt bad. MacFarlane had organised a man from
Scottish Water to go down with Sev. He introduced
himself as Stewart and indicated a pile of gear for Sev
to put on; overalls, thigh waders, miner's head lamps
and breathing apparatus.

'Enough air for forty minutes,' he told Sev.

'I don't think . . .'

'Health and Safety,' the guy insisted.

Sev shut up and pulled on the gear. He'd trained
down here with the Brigade and knew the score.

Sev went first, waiting until Stewart reached the
bottom rung of the ladder before setting off along
the sewer. The sewer had been checked by sniffer
dogs but the variety of pungent smells that lingered
here would have put anyone or anything off the scent.

Fifty metres further on, Sev spotted the first of the connecting drains on the opposite wall. He waited for his companion to catch up, then jumped across.

He was exiting the last one when a series of bangs went off. Stewart threw himself against the wall.

MacFarlane buzzed his mobile.

'Sorry about the noise. A couple of silly buggers throwing bangers on the brazier outside the first aid tent.'

'It's good to know you're in control, MacFarlane.'

MacFarlane ignored the sarcasm. 'Any luck?'

'Nothing.'

'It's heaving up here, though why anyone wants to dance a Strip the Willow up and down George Street in the middle of winter defeats me.'

'I can hear a siren.'

'Not coming here,' MacFarlane assured him. 'There's a concert due to start in half an hour on the Ross bandstand. You coming up for the show?'

'Wouldn't miss it for the world. Any sign of Rhona?'

'Nope. I've sent a car round to check out the flat where she's staying.'

'And find out the home number of that assistant she's so pally with. Maybe she's spoken to her recently.'

Sev signalled to a relieved Stewart that they should go back up. There was nothing more they could do down here. The immediate vicinity of the Gardens was clear. MacFarlane had arranged a high police presence. There were men on the roofs and the Brigade was on full alert.

When he reached the surface, Sev headed for a pub on Rose Street, where the bartender poured his usual without asking, while keeping one eye on the big screen in the corner.

Sev downed the double whisky in a oner, enjoying the kick. The one good thing about cutting down on the drink, he decided, was enjoying its effect again. He ordered another and had a look at what the rest of the pub was watching.

The crowds for the *Afore Fiesta* event exceeded even his expectations. A helicopter view was panning across the Gardens and the length of Princes Street. The events this year were designed to attract whole families. Sev was glad Gillian had deserted him and gone north with Amy. If she hadn't, Amy might have been out there now.

He pulled out his mobile and called his mother-in-law. It rang four times then the ansaphone kicked in. He resisted the temptation to curse into the mouthpiece. Gillian would love that on her mother's ansaphone. Instead he left a message for Amy and rang off. Wherever they were, they'd have to be back by Amy's bedtime. He would call again later.

He concentrated on the big screen, watching the crowd, looking for the face on the drawing. Every policeman out there had a copy of the sketch Jaz had done.

Sev ordered another drink. He went to throw it back then decided to make it last. He had a long night ahead.

When the mobile drilled ten minutes later, he thought it was Amy answering his message. It wasn't.

'Where the hell are you?' MacFarlane's voice was tense.

'Rose Street. Watching the telly.'

'I think you should get over here.'

22

THE WELL-DRESSED BLOND man looked embarrassed. Rhona told herself that intruders don't generally wear expensive Italian suits and stand in the hall looking mortified. The guy held out his hand.

'I'm sorry I startled you. Greg gave me a key.' He paused self consciously. 'We're seeing one another. He didn't tell you about me?'

'Of course he did.' Rhona assured him. 'You must be Justin.'

He looked relieved. 'Yes, I am.'

'Would you like to wait for Greg?'

He gave her a wide smile.

'Can I get you a coffee?'

'That would be great. Greg said he would be back about nine.'

When she came back with the coffee he'd settled himself on the settee. 'When Greg said you were staying, I must admit I was rather jealous.'

'I wouldn't worry about me,' she assured him. 'If there's one thing Greg's sure of it's his sexuality.'

He smiled. 'I hear you're a forensic scientist?'

'Yes.'

'Working on a case?'

'Always.'

Rhona wondered what age he was. Greg could certainly give him ten years. It was none of her business. Greg didn't mess in her sex life and she didn't mess in his. The secret of a long and happy friendship.

MacFarlane was in full flow when she reached the operations tent set up in the Gardens. It had taken half an hour to travel the short distance between Greg's flat and the end of Princes Street.

'Rhona!' MacRae grabbed her arm and led her in. 'We've been phoning everywhere for you.'

'Sorry.' Rhona was taken aback by MacRae's distracted appearance. 'I diverted my mobile while I was in the shower and Greg's ansaphone was on. What have I missed?'

MacFarlane pushed a piece of paper across the desk at her. MacRae was trying hard not to give her his own résumé as she read it. By the second paragraph she could see why. Right at the beginning, MacRae had planted the seed of doubt about Jaz. Everything on the paper suggested there were grounds for suspecting him.

'Well?'

She looked at MacRae. 'I don't believe it.'

'Why not?'

She hesitated, 'It doesn't feel right.'

'So speaks the true scientist,' MacRae pronounced.

MacFarlane took her side. 'Rhona's right. It's circumstantial.'

MacRae wasn't going to give up. 'He's been hanging about since the fire, sticking his nose in. He took the girl's dog, for God's sake. Psychological profiling of the arsonist suggests he will attempt to interject himself in the investigation because he feels safe enough to do so.'

MacRae took a breath before launching the next attack. 'Then you come up with the glad tidings that he served time with Robbie Stevens, the drug addict burned to death in the housing scheme arson attack. In fact they were cosier than that. They ended up inside together because they'd been running a nice little thieving business to feed their habits.'

'As far as we know Jaz has been clean since he got out,' MacFarlane said.

'Oh yeah? Then try this scenario for size. Jaz fancies the girl but she doesn't fancy him. He finds out where she's sleeping, rapes her then fires the place.'

'Okay,' MacFarlane came back, 'but you said the four fires in commercial property were lit by the same person.'

'It looks like it, but you can never be sure.' MacRae admitted grudgingly.

'You were sure,' Rhona said. 'And why link Jaz with Robbie Stevens' death? The arsonist is a professional. Why would he bother firing some poxy little flat in a housing scheme to get rid of a drug addict?'

MacRae glared at her. 'Maybe Jaz and Robbie were still working together. Maybe Robbie was messing him about. Maybe Jaz was working for someone else who wanted rid of Robbie. Who the fuck knows?'

Rhona was thinking back to her conversation with Jaz in the flat. The way he had sought her out, wanting her to put pressure on MacRae to get back on the case; wanting to find those responsible for Karen's death.

Why would he do that if he'd started the fire? Rhona didn't like thinking about the answer. Jaz could have given her a drawing of anyone, or of someone he didn't like. He could be diverting them from the real culprit . . . himself. But she had liked him. The dog trusted him.

'There's one way to find out if Jaz was involved,' she said.

'What?' MacRae came in.

'Bring him in, ask him to give a DNA sample. We can check it against the girl and the letter.'

They both looked at MacFarlane.

'There's one problem,' he said. 'Jaz and the dog have disappeared.'

'Since when?' MacRae asked.

'He was last seen on his pitch at Waverley Station yesterday morning,' MacFarlane said. 'The folk at the coffee bar and WH Smith's say he's regular as clock-work. He wasn't on his pitch today although a guard said he spotted him on the platform of a northbound train. We haven't been able to confirm that.'

'I saw Gillian and Amy off this morning,' MacRae said, looking worried.

The pieces were beginning to fit together, whether Rhona liked it or not. Jaz's preoccupation with getting MacRae back on the case. He'd been watching Gillian's house. He knew about the petrol bomb. It seemed so obvious. Jaz had tried to find out if she knew where Gillian and Amy were going. She had told him they were going north to stay with Amy's grandmother. They were going by train because Amy liked trains.

She'd spelt it out for him.

They were waiting for her to finish, MacRae's face already showing his worst fears had been confirmed.

'He's followed Gillian and Amy north,' she said.

23

THE BACK DOOR of the cottage swung open, exposing Jaz in a long streak of electric light. He pressed himself against the wall, his heart pounding.

The cottage was mocking in its silence. No long howl from Tommy, no sudden flash of steel at his face.

When he finally had the courage to go in, the hall was strangely welcoming, as if someone might emerge at any moment and say 'Hi'. In the kitchen three cups sat on the table, the teapot to hand. Beside the old-fashioned range Bess's basket lay waiting for her return.

Jaz trailed from room to room. They were all the same. Lived-in. Everything as it should be, except for the open front door and the blood-soaked body of the dead dog on the grass outside.

Jaz walked round the downstairs one more time then went back to the kitchen, lifted the blanket from Bess's basket and went outside.

He threw the blanket over Bess's body, silently cursing Tommy Moffat. The labrador was far too old to be a threat to anyone. She could bark, but that was about all. Which is probably why she died. Jaz had to stop himself picturing Emps lying somewhere between the cottage and the barn in exactly the same state. Tommy Moffat was a heid-banger, a nasty, twisted, creepy bastard. He would get him for this.

Jaz tucked his throbbing hand inside his coat and set off to check the drive and the garage for the car. Both were filled with nothing but shadows.

Where the fuck were they? Where was Tommy? Jaz didn't have an answer. He decided that standing outside freezing wasn't making him think any better.

Back in the cottage, he filled the kettle and pulled it over the hot ring to boil, then looked for the coffee. While he clutched the cup and thawed out, he thought about phoning the police. If they came and found the dead dog and the open front door, they would look for the occupants. If the police got involved they'd find his fingerprints all over the house. They would come looking for him. If Tommy had done something to the kid or the women, suspicion would be bound to fall on him.

With any luck, Amy and her mum had gone out before Tommy arrived. Tommy might have found the place empty, got pissed off and killed the dog. Jaz was warming to this version of events. Maybe Tommy never came to the cottage in the first place. Maybe someone else killed the dog. Jaz rinsed his cup at the sink and put it back where he got it, his mind made up.

The phone in the hall had the call light flashing. He pulled his cuff down to cover his finger and pressed the play button. MacRae's voice was gruff and Jaz could have sworn he heard a muffled curse before the message. MacRae wasn't pleased to find no one at home and said he would call back later.

Jaz dialled 1471, wrote the number on the telephone pad, tore it off and stuck it in his pocket. He would look for Tommy first, then contact MacRae. Jaz wasn't sure who he was more frightened of Tommy Moffat, or MacRae when he found out his kid was missing.

Outside, the moon was filling the back garden with silver light. Jaz struggled over the fence, cursing as pain shot through his mangled right hand, and set off into the wood.

MacRae flung the phone on the desk. 'If that punk's gone anywhere near Amy, I'll kill him.'

'Hold on, Sev,' Rhona tried. 'Is there any reason why Amy and Gillian wouldn't be at the cottage? Could they have gone out somewhere?'

'Where, for Chrissake?'

'Visiting a neighbour?'

MacRae was making a concentrated effort not to shout at her.

'Amy talked about watching the Hogmanay celebrations.'

Rhona looked at him. 'Sky!'

'Gillian's mother doesn't have Sky.'

'So maybe they went somewhere that did?'

MacRae looked stricken. 'I don't know anyone up there. I don't know where to phone and find out.'

Rhona looked at MacFarlane and he nodded imperceptibly.

'We'll send a car to check the cottage,' he said to MacRae. 'Then we'll make some enquiries. It's a rural area. Probably everyone within a twenty-mile radius will know where Gillian and Amy are tonight.'

The café was half-empty. Rhona went to the counter and brought back two mugs of scaldingly hot tea. MacRae was sitting at the same table they'd used at their first meeting.

'Knew you'd want to be near the Ladies,' he said.

'After you drink this, you'll want to be near the Gents.'

They sat in silence. Rhona could hear the distant music, a fast reel that got faster by the minute. In a few minutes the dance would stop and the concert begin. Maybe MacRae had been right all along. Maybe it was a hoax and the Torch, as Sev had taken to calling him, never intended to target tonight or any other night in the celebrations. Maybe he just wanted them running around thinking he would.

A different kind of music was signalling the start of the concert. Different from the mad whirl of fiddle and bagpipe, this was a soaring sound. Hauntingly Celtic.

MacRae checked his mobile.

'MacFarlane will contact us as soon as he has word about Amy,' Rhona assured him.

'I think I'll head up there tomorrow.'

'Good idea.'

'Assuming all goes well tonight.'

'It will,' Rhona said with a certainty she wasn't sure she felt. 'I think you were right,' she answered the cynical look. 'I think he wanted to put the wind up us. That's all.'

'He succeeded.'

The ring of the mobile stopped whatever MacRae planned to say next. Rhona watched his relief as he listened to the message. He slipped the mobile back in his pocket.

'Gillian and Amy are at the hotel with the rest of the village, watching the concert on the big screen. Gillian says they're fine and she'll phone in the morning.'

He reached for the half bottle in his pocket and threw some into his tea. 'The local policeman says no one fitting Jaz's description has been seen in the village, but he'll keep a lookout.'

'Jaz isn't a killer.'

'Then where is he?' He wanted her to give him an explanation he could believe.

'Maybe he needed to disappear for a while. Maybe he was getting on someone's nerves, asking all those questions, poking his nose in,' she suggested. 'He may be involved in the drug fires, but I don't think he's the Torch.'

'Neither do I,' he conceded at last. 'It takes a special kind of hatred for that.'

An ugly thought struck Rhona.

'If there is some connection between him and Robbie Stevens . . .'. She met Sev's eye. Jaz was moving from being the villain to being the hunted in both their minds.

MacRae stood up. 'Fancy some fresh air?'

They cut up into George Street. The crowd had dispersed, the dance billed as 'the longest Strip the Willow in the world' was over. The big, old-fashioned clock that hung above the door of Ottakars showed eleven o'clock.

'I could walk you back to Greg's,' MacRae offered.

'Maybe we should hang around a bit longer?'

'MacFarlane will get in touch if we're needed.'

They walked in a comfortable silence. The air was sharp, the pavement sparkling with frost. The sound of the concert faded. They skirted Charlotte Square and went along Shandwick Place. Rhona wondered, not for the first time, what Severino MacRae would be like off the job. Then she wondered if he ever was off the job. He put the job before everything, like she did.

By the time they reached the flat, cars were filling the westbound carriageway with families heading home. Rhona could tell by the set of MacRae's shoulders he was relaxing. She felt the same. Above them Greg's windows were in darkness. She suddenly didn't want to walk into an empty flat. MacRae must have guessed what she was thinking.

'I could do with a coffee,' he said.

He was sitting with his back to her, watching the fire. Rhona sat the coffee on the table then on an impulse fetched the whisky decanter from the cabinet.

MacRae accepted the glass without comment and moved over so she could sit next to him on the sofa.

'One down. Two to go.' He lifted his glass.

'I don't think Greg'll be happy if we finish his whisky.'

'You know what I mean.' His voice softened.

He moved his face close to hers.

'We make a good team,' he said gently.

He watched her reaction, his eyes bright blue in the firelight. Time hung for a moment between them, then he ran his finger gently down her cheek.

'So what happens now?' he said.

The sound of the siren woke her. Rhona rolled over, searching for the light switch. The ambulance screamed past and the room dropped back into silence. She glanced at the clock. She hadn't heard Greg come in. For a moment she thought about visiting his room to check, then decided against it in case the boyfriend was curled up in bed beside him.

'Hey.' MacRae was standing at the door.

'Hey.'

'You couldn't point me in the direction of the shower?'

'Three doors down on the left,' she said.

'Thanks.' MacRae smiled wryly. 'And by the way, the couch was as comfortable as you said it would be.'

Turning him down had been harder than Rhona could ever have imagined. It was a classic scenario; those who get frightened together, end up in bed together. And she didn't want to go there.

He'd taken the rejection well. Maybe too well for her ego. When he reappeared she was in the kitchen, coffee at the ready. He sat opposite her and proceeded to take in the designer surroundings.

'Don't say a word,' she warned him.

'I wouldn't dream of it,' he answered sweetly. 'Where's the owner?'

'If he's not asleep next door then he's with his latest, who gave me a hell of a fright last night by appearing from nowhere. He's got a key, so it must be serious.'

They lapsed into silence, Rhona trying to keep her mind off what the morning might have been.

'So what happens now?' she said.

'We've had that conversation. You turned me down, remember?'

Rhona changed the subject. 'You said you were going north.'

MacRae's face darkened. 'I've decided against it. Gillian and I would only argue in front of Amy and I don't want that. Anyway, the Hogmanay celebrations aren't over yet.'

Two days still to go.

'I can hang around here if it helps?'

'Better get back to your own murder. Knowing the mean city there will be plenty of forensic work for you over the next couple of days.'

Glasgow at Hogmanay. A whole year's Friday and Saturday nights rolled into one. Sentimentality and violence walking hand in hand. A lethal combination.

They parted company at the door. MacRae didn't look back as he went down the stairs. He was trouble, in more ways than one.

It took an hour to pack and tidy up. She eventually knocked on Greg's bedroom door and glanced inside. The bed hadn't been slept in. He must have spent the night at Justin's. Rhona wondered if she should call him, then decided to leave a thank you note instead.

The journey back was uneventful. The clear cold skies clouded over as she neared Harthill, bringing thick sleet against the window.

A text message came in ten minutes later, making her heart skip a beat.

*Hillhead Underground 8? Lia*m

She texted back *Yes*.

24

THE MOTORBIKE WASN'T difficult to trace. The girl in the petrol station at the village was only too glad to talk about it. Jaz emerged with a can of Coke and a sandwich, some paracetamol, an invitation to a party and exactly what he wanted to know. The whereabouts of Tommy Moffat.

Tommy had arrived at the petrol station at about nine. Jaz imagined the girl's paroxysms of delight that someone with a cool motorbike was planning to spend Hogmanay in the village. He'd asked for somewhere to stay and she'd suggested her mum's Bed and Breakfast. Tommy had agreed and then asked her what he really wanted to know, where Skiach Lodge was. She had given him directions.

Jaz hadn't made quite the same impact. No motorbike and no cool gear, but she'd invited him to the party anyway. After all, tomorrow was Hogmanay.

Frost was forming on the road and now and then a sliver of frozen rain hit his face. Jaz passed a hotel bar loud with convivial voices. A kid pushed the door open and rushed outside, another kid following. They swung in a cold circle then dashed back in. Jaz almost followed them into the blast of warmth and good humour.

At the end of a string of houses, the road forked. Skiach Lodge was on the left hand fork.

As he passed the last street lamp, the way ahead grew murky. The pavement dwindled to a narrow track between the tar and the bordering trees. Jaz stumbled along, wondering if it was raining as hard in Edinburgh. MacRae would like that, he decided. It would put a damper on the whole proceedings. Jaz swung his thoughts away from MacRae and the woman forensic. He had his own job to do.

Skiach Lodge was well-hidden by trees, protected from the gaze of the casual passer-by. Jaz was over the wall and into the dense, wet undergrowth of wintering rhododendrons. He was soaked through and the bitter wind clawed at him. Whatever happened, he had to find shelter soon.

He made for the back entrance. A gate led through a high wall into ridges of frozen soil. Ahead, a kitchen window shone a welcome. Jaz kept hard against the wall and risked a look.

He had to admit the bastard looked at home. His feet were up on the fender, a can of lager at his mouth. Jaz wanted to crush the can down Tommy's throat. He clenched his teeth and listened.

Tommy was talking to somebody. Jaz couldn't see who it was but he knew it was female. Tommy was on his feet now, thrusting his tight-jeaned hips forward to show off the hard dick. The girl came into view. She was getting the message alright. She slipped between Tommy and the kitchen table. Tommy drained the last drop of his can and pulled down his zip.

Tommy was fully occupied. Jaz took the chance to get inside unnoticed.

He found himself in a narrow passageway. A door to the left lay ajar, revealing steps down to the basement. The sound of grunts and moans came from the kitchen. Jaz kept going down the passageway and found himself in a grand entrance hall with a sweeping staircase.

Behind him Tommy and his partner were reaching their climax. The girl must like living dangerously. On the last, long drawn out groan, a set of double doors on the opposite wall were pulled open. Jaz hid in the shadows as a man in a suit headed for the kitchen.

Tommy appeared minutes later, adjusting his zip, a smug grin on his face. There was a shouted greeting, then the double doors shut behind him. Jaz crept closer to listen.

By the time he left, Jaz was dry again. The basement steps had led to a boiler, on at full blast. He cleared a place behind it and settled down to dry out. After that he would check back at the cottage, see if Amy was back. Then he would look for Emps.

Judging by the conversation he'd tuned into, Tommy would soon be heading for the garage and his next shag. Just as well. With the information he'd overheard, Moffat had better get all the normal sex he could. Once Jaz made sure he was banged up inside, sex would take on a different hue.

The rain had stopped, and above him the sky was clear and midnight blue. Now that he had moonlight

Jaz found his way out of the grounds quickly. Five minutes along the main road he thought he heard a motorbike and threw himself into the ditch, soaking his feet again, but it was only a diesel van with a bad exhaust.

The hotel party had quietened down. There were only three vehicles left outside. Jaz took a chance and went in.

In the bar, Jaz ordered a pint and a hot pie and found a seat close to the fire. His injured hand was swollen and useless, and he had to rely on his teeth to open the paracetamol packet. He gulped down two tablets with his beer. He spotted Amy when she came out of the toilet behind her mum and turned away, relieved to see her unharmed but already thinking about what she would find when she got back to the cottage.

Jaz drained his pint and contemplated another. He had a look in his wallet. Not much chance of a Bed and Breakfast. He thought about asking if he could clear up the bar, wash all the glasses in exchange for bedding down beside the fire, but the barman didn't look the benevolent type. The last thing he wanted was to become an item for gossip. It would be better if Tommy thought he had left the area. Jaz shifted in the warm seat. Better hit the cold now before he got too comfortable.

He went to the bar and asked for another pie to take away. The barman put it in a bag for him along with the two remaining sausage rolls. He waved away payment and went back to the glasses. Jaz nodded his thanks and made for the door before he changed his mind and asked to stay.

Outside the cold was like a vice. Jaz pulled up his hood. Now that he knew Amy was alright, he would go straight to the barn. With any luck Emps would head back there looking for him . . . if he was alive. Jaz could only pray he was.

Even the piled hay in the barn couldn't keep the chill out of his bones. At dawn Jaz stood up and walked about, stamping the circulation back into his feet and throwing his good arm round his body. He would give it an hour, then try and hitch a lift back into town.

He fished the sausage rolls out of his pocket and wolfed them down, dreaming of a mug of hot tea.

The fields were covered with a layer of frost and an early sun was sending thin shivering rays across the empty furrows. Jaz suddenly remembered the significance of the day. Hogmanay. Tomorrow was a new year and a new start. Maybe for him, when he sorted things out. But not for Karen.

He heard the dog before he saw it; the sound of paws clipping the icy puddles that covered the churned mud round the barn. There was a strangled noise of excitement, then Emps was on him.

So there was a God, after all.

Jaz tried to hug the dog, but he yelped and leapt away.

'Whoa! What's up, Emps?'

The dog came back, twisting its back legs from side to side in a mockery of the missing tail.

Jaz gazed in horror at the mutilated and bleeding stump, while Emps licked the salty tears that ran down his face.

'I'll get him Emps. I promise. And when I get him I'll cut off his fuckin' dick and stick it down his fuckin' throat.'

25

BILL HAD BEEN true to his word. Rhona studied the contents of the forensic bags. If the body on the moor was that of the paedophile and murderer they'd been searching for for the last six months, it would lay her fears to rest. She could stop looking for him in the street, stop imagining she would wake up one night and find him standing at the foot of her bed.

Chrissy was watching her. 'I can deal with these,' she offered.

'I'd rather do it myself.'

Rhona pulled on her lab coat.

'But it's Hogmanay.'

'I'll be away by eight, I promise.'

Chrissy gave up. 'I've had a look at the fire video.'

'And?'

'The guy you talked about . . .'

'In the drawing?'

'No. Your fire investigator.'

'MacRae?' Rhona was puzzled.

'What does he look like?' Chrissy asked.

'He's about five eleven, dark hair, part Italian . . .'

'Does he wear a black leather jacket?' Chrissy asked.

'Yes, why?'

'Take a look at this.' Chrissy handed Rhona the remote.

He was standing on the edge of the crowd looking up. Rhona paused the video and stared. The resemblance was uncanny, but the video was of a Glasgow fire forty-six miles away from MacRae's territory.

'It can't be him,' Rhona said to convince herself.

'It looks like him then?'

Rhona nodded.

'Quite tasty.'

'He's badly scarred.' Rhona regretted the words as soon as they were out.

Chrissy looked interested. 'Really? Where?'

'Chrissy,' Rhona warned.

Chrissy raised her eyebrows.

'What makes you think it's not him?'

'He would have said if he'd been at the Glasgow fire.'

'Especially if he started it.'

'Don't be ridiculous.'

Chrissy ejected the video and replaced it with another and pressed rewind. She waited a moment then froze it.

'Take a look on the left.'

Rhona's heart missed a beat.

'Would you believe it?' Chrissy said. 'Old leather jacket's back again.'

The figure was further away from the camera this time making it more difficult to make out his features.

'I spotted him or someone who looks like him in three out of the last four.'

'There must be an explanation.'

'As to why MacRae keeps popping up in our fire videos?'

'It's not him,' Rhona was adamant. 'It's someone who looks like him, or,' she said with more certainty this time, 'someone who chooses to look like him.'

'Neat idea. A MacRae lookalike visiting fire scenes.'

'You didn't see anyone who looked like Jaz's drawing?'

Chrissy shook her head. 'What about the Edinburgh footage?'

Rhona went for her bag.

'That's funny.'

'What?'

'I put the video in the zipped pocket but now it's in the main part.'

'You took it out, watched it and put it back in a different pouch?' Chrissy suggested.

'I haven't had time to watch it.'

Rhona slipped in the Edinburgh footage. The fire that blazed on the screen was well established, already consuming the lower levels of the Princes Street building, spreading rapidly in a horizontal direction.

Since the building had been lying empty with few combustible linings and interior contents, the use of accelerants looked likely from observation alone, though the speed and action of the fire was not what Rhona was looking at.

She concentrated on the shots of the watching crowd. The perpetrator could often be standing within yards of the firefighters, watching them risk their lives dealing with their handiwork.

Rhona ran the footage four times.

'He's not there,' Chrissy said at last.

'No, he's not.'

The fire had started in the early hours of the morning when few people were about. The crowds were smaller than would be expected for such a spectacular blaze.

'The arsonist must have been disappointed by the turnout,' Rhona said. 'No wonder he threatened the New Year celebrations.'

'What?'

She explained about the letters, without mentioning her place in them.

Chrissy looked puzzled. 'You think the two spates of fire-raising are connected?'

'Yes. Though I have no real proof. I'm going to take a look through the most recent reports. There might be something I've missed.'

'Now?' Chrissy was incredulous. Four o'clock in the afternoon seemed a bad time to start wading through five detailed forensic reports. 'I take it Sean's not in town?'

'A gig in Amsterdam.'

'You should have stayed in Edinburgh with your tasty Italian,' was Chrissy's parting shot when she left at five.

Rhona hoped that was Chrissy's idea of a joke and she hadn't been reading her mind.

Rhona settled at her desk, resisting the temptation to try and get a hold of Bill Wilson and talk things through with him. If Bill had any sense he would be home with his family for Hogmanay. She selected one of the reports, thick with the minutiae of death, and set to work.

When her mobile alarm warned her it was quarter to eight, she had already trawled through three reports she had verified and signed some time in the last six months. The evidence suggested the fires had been started deliberately or were the result of extreme carelessness on the part of the victim, who was either a known or suspected member of the drug scene. There were no suspects for any of them.

She shelved the reports and locked up.

Outside, her breath met the air in a vaporised cloud. The security guard at the gate waved cheerio from the warmth of his box and shouted his good wishes for Hogmanay.

She decided to leave the car in the university car park. Hillhead underground station was only minutes away. To her left, the Gothic towers of the university loomed out of the darkness. The surrounding shrubbery was shrouded in shadow. The click of her footsteps on the frosty pavement seemed to echo her rapid heartbeat.

She was going to see her son for the first time in eighteen years. The tiny baby she had given up for adoption was a young man now. Would he look like her or Edward? What if he was like Edward in character? Then they might grow to hate one another. Rhona found herself slowing down. Maybe this wasn't a good idea after all.

Byres Road was busy, early revellers pouring in and out of the most popular bars.

A tall familiar figure stood outside the underground station, causing Rhona to stop in her tracks.

Three drunks wearing kilts and Scotland tops emerged, singing *Flower of Scotland* and she momentarily lost sight of him. Then he reappeared, threw her a half-smile and turned swiftly in at the underground entrance. A wave of revulsion swept over Rhona. It couldn't be him. He was dead. It was only a matter of time before it was confirmed. It had to be someone who looked like him. It was that horrible half-smile. That and her own private horror of ever seeing him again.

She pulled herself together. You can't see someone who's dead, she told herself. Not unless you believe in ghosts.

Her watch said ten past eight. The thought crept into her mind that Liam wasn't going to show. She waited for another twenty minutes then with a heavy heart sent a *Missed you. Please call* text message and went home.

Back in the empty flat she contemplated phoning Sean. She lifted the receiver then replaced it. If she spoke to him now he would know something was wrong and she couldn't bear to tell him that Liam hadn't turned up.

She wandered through the flat, talking to herself, hating the solitude she had once loved. Sharing her flat with Sean had destroyed her ability to be alone. She had never felt lonely in her home before him. Alone yes, lonely never.

She heard a noise and jumped, her nerves on edge, but it was only the cat come looking for food.

Once she'd fed it, she listened to the radio while making something for herself. Both Edinburgh and Glasgow were well into their New Year celebrations. Everything was going accordingly to plan. She imagined MacFarlane's relief . . . and Sev's.

'We make a good team,' he'd said.

The buzzer went at 11.30. She had switched on the television and poured a drink to toast the bells.

'Can I come up?'

Rhona pressed the door release and let him in, shocked by the pleasure that had rushed through her at the sound of his voice.

His eyes were heavily shadowed but there was no smell of alcohol on his breath. She led him through to the sitting room, saying nothing.

'All alone?'

She nodded.

'Where's the boyfriend?'

'Amsterdam.'

He was watching her face, reading the pain.

'What's up?' he said softly, intimately.

When she didn't answer, he took her in his arms and held her close.

'I hate fucking Hogmanay,' he said.

She breathed out against him. 'So do I.'

The phone rang in the hall.

'Leave it,' he told her.

26

BILL CALLED HER early to tell her about the car. Rhona listened, her head still stupid with sleep and too much whisky.

'I don't understand.'

'I tried to get you late last night, but you weren't answering. Chrissy came back to the lab to ask you to go for a drink. She saw your car go up in flames and thought you were in it. She tried to open the door.'

'My God! Is she alright?'

'Burned her hands but otherwise, yes, she's alright. She's in the Western Infirmary.'

'I'll get a taxi there right away. Oh, and Bill . . . where's my car?'

'They've taken it to the police garage. A team is checking it over.'

In the sitting-room the blanket and pillows she'd given Severino were folded at the end of the couch. An empty whisky bottle and two glasses stared reproachfully back at her from the table, a note beside them. He had gone for a walk to clear his head and would phone later.

Rhona was relieved not to have to face him.

The receptionist in Accident & Emergency directed

her to Ward Three. Chrissy was asleep when she went in. Rhona searched the pale face for burns. It was unmarked, but the hands . . .

'Oh Chrissy,' she whispered, distressed.

Chrissy opened her eyes.

'I thought you were asleep.'

'I have to pretend, or that Sister will take my temperature again.' She winced as she tried to pull herself up in bed.

'What's going on, Rhona?'

'I don't know.'

'If you ask me, someone's got it in for you.'

'It might have been an accident. We don't know yet.'

Chrissy wasn't convinced.

'Are you going to examine the car?'

Rhona nodded. 'I'm going there now.'

Chrissy was trying to get out of bed.

'Where do you think you're going?'

'With you.'

'Oh no you're not. You're staying here until they say you can leave.'

'But . . .'

Rhona held up her hand. 'No buts.'

'No evidence of a timing device?' Bill asked.

Rhona shook her head.

'But definitely arson?'

She nodded. 'The fire started in the passenger compartment. They identified two different sources of ignition.'

After she'd talked to the SOCOs and taken a look at

the car herself, she'd gone in search of Bill. The car was in a mess, but the quick use of a fire extinguisher by the security guard had confined the fire to the front two seats.

'Was there anything that might point to the identity of the arsonist?'

'There was a tin on the driver's seat with a photograph of me in it and an audio tape of the Stones singing *Jumping Jack Flash*.'

'I take it not belonging to you?'

She nodded. 'And someone left a song about fire on my ansaphone last week . . .'

Bill's voice grew serious.

'I don't like this, Rhona.'

Neither did she.

'Maybe the security cameras can throw some light on it. I've got someone ploughing through the footage now.' He looked at her, concerned. 'Is Sean about?'

'Amsterdam,' she told him.

He was obviously worried about her. 'I'll get a squad car to drop you home.'

She conceded that, at least.

'My advice is to stay home,' he told her. 'I'll let you know when we have anything.'

Rhona pressed the play button on the recorder. Mick Jagger's distinctive voice filled the room, the thump of bass guitar behind it.

'*Jumping Jack Flash*, the Rolling Stones, 1969 or '70,' Sev told her.

'I know.'

'So?'

'My car was set on fire last night after I left the lab. Whoever did it left a photo of me in the car, and that tape.'

There was a moment's silence as he digested that. Then she voiced her fear.

'It could mean he's planning to use propane.'

27

BILL WILSON HURRIED back to the police office. He'd
promised his wife Margaret he would be back by three
to serve the elderly relatives their Ne'erday dram, and
he intended keeping his promise. The empty streets
looked like a Sunday with a hangover. A few souls were
wandering about looking for the remains of a party, but
the rest were indoors continuing the celebrations or
sleeping it off.

Janice had been one of the ones to draw the short
straw and work Hogmanay. She'd taken the news well.
She wasn't a big drinker anyway. When the team went
for a pint after a shift, her limit seemed to be two
glasses of wine.

Janice wasn't at her desk but there was a large yellow
notelet on his. Some guy had phoned and said he knew
Dr MacLeod and wanted to speak to the man in charge
of the drug murders. He had refused to talk to anyone
else.

Bill carried his over-milked coffee to his room and
sat on his leather swivel chair to think.

'So you're back.'

Janice made it sound as if he was a kid skiving class.
Bill waved the note at her.

'Don't know who it was,' she said. 'Sounded jumpy and would only speak to you. I could hear a dog whining in the background.'

'If he calls back, I want it traced.'

'We're short-staffed but I'll try. And, sir. The report on Meldrum Holdings is ready.'

Despite being down to three men and a dog, Janice had achieved the impossible. DI Wilson felt suitably chastened.

The report was ten pages long. Meldrum Holdings were wide-ranging in their interests, from construction to financial services to manufacturing. It would need a complicated flow chart to signal where the money came from and where it went. When regions had their own direct services it was easy enough to spot where the money went – down a black hole. Now that the private sector had been brought in for the construction and maintenance of public housing, things were a little less clear.

Meldrum Holdings looked as though they were doing a nice job of bulldozing run-down schemes. Now if they were doing a nice wee job of redeveloping them as well . . .

When he left at two, Bill was none the wiser. Linking anyone in Meldrum Holdings to arson in housing estates would be like coming up with the correct string of lottery numbers, and just about as pleasurable.

On his way home he took a detour. One of those things that happens on the Kingston Bridge, Bill convinced himself, trying to blot out the expression on

Margaret's face when he didn't arrive. He rehearsed his excuses. He was dreaming and ended up in the wrong lane and had to keep going to the next junction, before he could get off.

Minutes later the slip road he'd chosen deposited him in a desert of high-rise flats and creeping waste-land. The pub was on a corner, between the bookies and the post office-cum-general store.

No one in the pub looked at him but they all saw him. He went and sat at the bar.

'Happy New Year, Sarge,' said the balding, hollow-cheeked man next to him.

Wee Archie didn't believe in promotion. If he wasn't moving up in the world, then no one else was.

'Happy New Year, Archie.'

Bill nodded at the barman and Archie had his whisky and half pint replenished.

Archie had lived in this housing scheme all his life. He'd seen it begin good and end up bad. If anyone knew what was going on here, it was him.

It took two more shorts before Archie's brain went into play.

28

JAZ PUT DOWN the receiver and stepped out of the phone booth into the wind.

No trains, no boats, no planes out of Auchenblair on New Year's Day. He'd tried to hitch but nobody was driving anywhere other than round the corner and Jaz didn't fancy the hike to the main road for a lorry heading south. So he'd tried phoning. Except there was no MacRae and no MacFarlane and now no DI Wilson around. The lady scientist had been his last chance. He wasn't too happy about Emps either. The dog's nose was hot, and he kept whining. Worrying about Emps' pain made him forget his own.

The hills behind the village were white-topped and the sky hung heavy with snow. He decided to go to the hotel bar. There was no point holding on to cash for the train now. He would blow it on something to eat and a heat by the fire.

Amy jumped the two steps from the blue front door and landed right in front of him.

'What happened to Emperor?'

Emps was licking the wee girl's hand.

'He got his tail caught in a door.'

'You'll have to take him to the vet.'

'I will,' Jaz promised, 'as soon as I get back to Edinburgh.'

'Why don't you go now?' Amy looked horrified at the sight of the seeping stump.

'No transport until tomorrow,' he explained.

Mrs MacRae had appeared at the door.

Amy ran back up the steps. 'Mummy, Emps got hurt and he can't go to the vet until tomorrow. Granny could help him, couldn't she?'

Mrs MacRae was giving Jaz one of her 'Who the hell are you?' looks.

'It's okay, Amy,' Jaz was anxious to be away. 'Emps will be okay.'

Jaz made to walk on but Mrs MacRae had bent down to examine the dog's wound.

'What if Emperor dies like Bess?' Amy turned to Jaz. 'Bess hurt herself on a fence when we were out. She died.' Tears filled her eyes.

So that's what they'd told her about the dog.

'Amy, go inside and say goodbye to Jennie. Tell her we'll see her tomorrow at the party.'

'But Mummy . . .'

'Go.'

MacRae's wife turned to him.

'This dog needs a vet.'

'I'm stuck here until tomorrow,' Jaz began.

'If you come home with us, my mother will look at him for you.'

Arguing didn't look like an option. And Emps did need to see a vet. Anyway, getting close to MacRae's wife and kid had been the reason he came here in the first place.

'Okay.'

Bess's body had been removed from the front lawn. Jaz tried not to look for bloodstains as he followed Amy up the path. He would insist on waiting outside, he decided, his stomach jumping in fright at the sudden thought of MacRae turning up on New Year's Day and finding him sitting in his mother-in-law's kitchen. Christ! He would end up with more than a hole in his hand.

Amy was running ahead, throwing open the door and calling to her gran to come and see the poor dog.

Jaz stopped at the door.

'I'll wait here.'

'Nonsense,' Mrs MacRae said. 'You'll need to hold Emperor while we dress his wound.'

Emperor was asleep now, knocked out by the anti-biotics he'd had pumped into him.

'You'd better leave Emps here so that I can keep an eye on him overnight.' Amy's gran topped up the mug of tea. 'Where are you staying?'

Jaz went through half a dozen scenarios in his head in quick succession then decided to opt for the truth, or nearly the truth.

'I expected to go back today,' he smiled ruefully, 'I forgot about the trains.'

'There's a room over the garage you can have for tonight.'

Mrs MacRae wasn't happy about the offer but a quick glance from her mother silenced her.

'It's not much, but it's warm and you can see Emperor first thing in the morning.'

'I don't want to put you to any trouble,' Jaz said.

'No trouble. The weather's closing in. You'd have problems going anywhere tonight.'

The four-paned kitchen window was thick with snow. Amy left her place by Emperor and ran over to the window in delight.

'Can I phone Dad and tell him?'

Jaz's heart sank. The first thing Amy would do was tell her father that Emperor was in the house. Then it would all be over. The police car would be here in minutes.

'Can I use your toilet?' Jaz asked quickly. He would have to leave Emps behind, but the dog was better off here, the state he was in.

'It's through the back,' MacRae's wife had the kitchen door open for him.

Amy was already dialling. Jaz listened from the hall. He could feel the wee girl's impatience as she waited for someone to pick up.

'Never mind Amy,' her mother was saying. 'Your dad'll be working. You can try again tomorrow.'

Jaz went into the bathroom and flushed the toilet. Maybe he would get a sleep in a bed tonight after all. As long as he was away sharp in the morning.

The room over the garage was used for storage, but the bed was comfortable and wonderfully warm. After showering he put his clothes back on and left his parka at the foot of the bed and climbed in.

When he left the kitchen, Emperor hadn't stirred from his deep sleep beside the range. The old woman had listened to the dog's heartbeat and pronounced his progress satisfactory. Nothing was said about his injuries or Bess's death. The old woman seemed to have accepted him at face value, but her daughter was a different matter.

Jaz had caught her looking at him during supper and he was sure she didn't believe a word of his story. He had a feeling she had decided keeping him there might be the best idea, at least until she'd spoken to her husband or the police.

He was awakened two hours later by the thump of snow sliding off the garage roof. He slipped out of bed and reached for his jacket, deciding to check on Emperor.

The kitchen was in darkness apart from a small lamp near the Aga. Jaz bent over the dog, relieved to see the blanket rise and fall with gentle regularity.

'How's he doing?' Amy's gran was standing at the door in her dressing gown.

'Okay, I think.'

'Let's have a look.'

She lifted the heavy eyelids. 'The sedative should wear off soon. He'll be up and about by morning.'

'I want to thank you.'

'No need. It's my job.'

'But you usually get paid.'

'I'm retired. I like to keep my hand in.' She fetched two mugs from the cupboard. 'Emperor is very fond of you. Have you had him since he was a puppy?'

Jaz decided on the truth. 'He belonged to a friend who died.'

'I'm sorry.'

She lifted the boiling kettle and made a pot of tea.

'My daughter doesn't trust you.' She took a seat at the table. 'She wanted to phone the police after you went to bed.'

'What?' Jaz was on his feet.

The old woman waved him back to his seat. 'I told her not to,' she smiled. 'She still listens to me now and again.' She sipped her tea. 'I told her anyone who cared about their dog as much as you do couldn't be all bad.'

'Thanks. I'll be out of your way in the morning.'

She glanced at the window.

'You might be stuck with us a little longer than that. Snow has a habit of slowing the world down, sometimes for the better.'

Sitting in that kitchen drinking tea, watching the snow fall outside, was like being in a different universe. If the old woman wanted him to tell her his life story, the truth about Karen, why he was here, she was going the right way about it.

'I know who killed your dog.'

'Was it you who covered Bess with a blanket?'

He nodded and she waited for him to go on.

'A bloke called Tommy Moffat. He's a . . . well, he's a nutcase.'

'Why did he kill Bess?'

'Because he wanted to. Because he felt like it,' he said angrily. 'Who knows? Maybe she just barked and annoyed him.'

'Where is this Tommy Moffat now?'

'He's gone,' Jaz said, hoping that was true.

'Did he have anything to do with Emperor's tail and your hand?'

Jaz nodded.

'Can I take a look at it?'

He held it out.

'The wound's deep and quite inflamed. Would you let me dress it for you and give you a shot of anti-biotics?'

Jaz hesitated then nodded.

She poured hot water into a basin and carefully cleaned and dressed the wound. Then she pulled up his sleeve, exposing the old needle tracks.

She said nothing as she slid the needle into his arm.

'This might make you feel sleepy.'

'What if the police . . . ?'

'There will be no police here tonight.'

Jaz went back to his room and got into bed. The world outside was dark and silent, wrapped in a white cocoon. For the first time in forty-eight hours, Jaz felt safe.

29

WEE ARCHIE WAS a one-syllable man. Talking to him was a case of twenty questions. Bill Wilson was conscious he had reached nineteen and didn't have his answer yet.

One more question and Archie had had enough. He might be a drinker but he always went home for his mid-day meal. A happily married man, was Archie, and he wasn't going to miss his New Year lunch. When they got outside, he threw his parting shot as Bill got in the car.

'After our boy died, Marge was all for joining them. Somebody has to clean the place up,' he said angrily. 'Your lot aren't doing anything about it.'

If Archie's veiled suggestions were to be believed, clearing out drug pushers from the estate was a joint effort. Big business working with a local enterprise group. It was what the government would call a private-public partnership. The clean residents get rid of the junkies while big business makes a killing on the building and land deals. Bill wondered if the local vigilantes realised they would be the next to go.

On the way home, Bill phoned the hospital to check

on Chrissy. The ward sister said Chrissy was asleep
and sounded pleased about that. She would be dis-
charged in the morning. The sister didn't say 'Thank
God', but Bill could hear it in the tone of her voice.
Chrissy was not in the model patients' league.

He called Rhona's home number.

A sleepy Irish voice answered.

'Sean?'

'Hi Bill. Sorry, I'm half asleep.'

'Is Rhona there?'

'No. She doesn't even know I'm back. There was a
cancellation so I jumped a plane. She's been here
recently though. Looks like the remains of last night's
celebrations.'

Bill filled him in about the car fire.

'God, I had no idea this was all going on.' He
scrabbled about in the background. 'An urgent fax
arrived half an hour ago, something about coffee cups.
Do you want me to read it?'

The fax was two pages long. One was technical
gibberish to both of them. The second stated a match
between DNA residue on one of the cups submitted
and the semen residue on the letter.

'Have you tried her mobile?' Bill said.

'It's sitting in the recharger. I'm going to try Mrs
Harper downstairs. She might have spoken to Rhona
or seen her leave.'

When Sean rang off, Bill sat in his car trying to figure
out what the hell coffee cups had to do with anything. It
took five minutes for Sean to call back.

'Mrs Harper saw her leave with a dark-haired man in

a leather jacket about lunchtime,' Sean told him. 'She doesn't know if there was a car.'

'I'll go round by the hospital and check with Chrissy. See if she knows anything about the cups or this guy.'

Bill headed for the Infirmary. One thing was certain, if anyone knew the whole story it would be Chrissy. How much she would be prepared to reveal was a different matter. Chrissy took loyalty very seriously.

The ward sister threw him a look of relief when he arrived.

'She's up and about,' she said. 'Try the television room.'

Chrissy was in there trying to organise a game of cards with the other residents, who just wanted to watch an hour-long episode of *Eastenders*.

'DI Wilson. You've come to rescue me.'

She took him to the quiet room.

'The cup came from Greg's flat. Rhona took it from there after the boy with the dog turned up. MacRae put the wind up her about him,' she said. 'It's funny though, she told me the cup tested clean.'

'She had more than one cup tested.'

'Didn't know about that,' Chrissy looked puzzled. 'Why don't you ask Rhona?'

'We don't know where she is,' Bill told her. 'Her neighbour saw her go off with a dark-haired guy in a leather jacket about lunchtime.'

'What?' Chrissy sounded alarmed. 'There was a guy like that in the videos hanging about every fire. No clear facial image. Just the dark hair and the leather jacket. I told her it looked like MacRae.'

'I'll contact MacFarlane,' Bill reassured her. 'Chances are Rhona's in Edinburgh with them.'

'If the cup tested positive . . . then the boy with the dog must have sent the letter.'

'Yes,' said Bill, rising to leave.

Chrissy got up too. 'I'm coming with you.'

'You're not allowed out until tomorrow,' Bill tried.

'They'll be glad to see the tail-end of me.'

30

'JAZ DIDN'T HAVE anything to do with Karen's death.'

MacRae didn't turn his head from the snowy windscreen. He was waiting for her to prove what she said was true.

'When he came to the flat, I kept his coffee cup.'

He took his eyes off the road. 'What?'

'Careful!' The stretch of road at Harthill was renowned for its bad weather accidents.

The highest point between Glasgow and Edinburgh was the very place to come off the road in a snowstorm.

MacRae slowed down. 'Why?'

'I was worried he might have stolen something, so when he left I bagged the cup. When nothing was missing I forgot about it. Then you got suspicious about him so I analysed it. The DNA pattern didn't match either the letter or the semen in Karen.'

'I still don't trust him.'

'You don't trust anyone.'

MacRae grunted and swung left into Harthill Service Station.

'I want to phone Amy.'

★   ★   ★

Rhona waited for MacRae to return. She hadn't been completely honest with him. She'd removed three cups from Greg's flat. After Jaz left, she'd sat his cup by the sink. When MacRae threw suspicion on Jaz, she decided to test the cup. But there were three beside the sink by then and they all looked the same. One result was back.

'The line's down.' MacRae looked worried. 'Heavy snow.'

'Mobile?'

'No chance. They're surrounded by hills.'

'Amy'll be pleased.'

'What?'

'The snow.'

They looked out at the thickening cover.

'We'd better get moving,' she suggested.

Rhona was back in the car when she remembered.

'Shit!'

'What's up?'

'I've left my mobile and Greg's keys behind.'

MacRae didn't look round. 'No problem. I can get you in anywhere.'

Mary Queen of Scots' squat was littered with a fresh covering of empty lager cans. Either the Queen had taken up residence again or someone else had.

When they got to the manhole it was back in place.

'It's fucking padlocked,' MacRae looked at her in frustration.

'What about a car jack?'

*   *   *

The sewer was warm and damp. Rhona wondered why Mary Queen of Scots and her entourage hadn't made their home down here, away from the police and the cold. MacRae must have been reading her mind.

'Most people don't know this place exists.' He stopped and used the torch to check the map. 'I marked each of the side tunnels I checked out.' He pointed at the opposite wall. 'I think we're about level with the toilets at the western end of the Gardens.'

While they were walking their footsteps had played back at them, jumping across the tunnel walls, making them sound like an advancing army. Now they were standing still the echo that rang behind did not belong to them. Rhona was sure of it. She looked at MacRae and mouthed 'Keep talking'.

'I vote we head back,' she suggested loudly. 'We shouldn't be down here without the proper equipment anyway.'

The footsteps had stopped. If someone from Scottish Water was down there they would have made their presence known by now.

'Good idea,' MacRae shouted as Rhona took off.

The cobbled ledge rang beneath her feet. MacRae's breath rasped as he pounded along behind her. A distant thump was followed by the sound of splashing water. Disturbed silt propelled noxious gases into the air. Rhona coughed as they hit the back of her throat and flooded her eyes with water.

She upped her pace, praying she wouldn't miss her footing in the darkness and fall off the ledge. She swerved instinctively as the tunnel curved right but

MacRae didn't react so quickly. There was a crunch then a stream of curses as he collided with the wall.

Rhona's beam of light caught a foot as it slipped into a right-hand tunnel. She jumped across the channel and looked down the side sewer. Nothing. It sounded as though her quarry had gone to ground or else found a way out.

Rhona, head well down, entered the side tunnel, hearing MacRae cross, gasping for breath, behind her.

Ahead, a dark shape blocked the tunnel. She stepped closer and the smell of death hit her like an intervening wall. Bending down, she examined the body. A week of heat and damp had decomposed it beyond all recognition.

Somewhere in the distance, she heard feet clamber up metal steps. A gush of noise and fresh air signalled an escape into the Gardens.

MacRae was coming towards her, bent double.

'Christ, something smells bad.'

He peered past her.

'Anyone we know?'

'I'd say the guy in the drawing. Hair colour and clothes are the same and he's wearing a nose ring.'

'No wonder the police couldn't find him. Did you see who we were chasing?'

'I saw a man's shoe in the torchlight. Brown . . . black . . . I'm not sure.'

'You're shivering.'

'I'm fine,' she lied.

'Let's get out of here. There's an exit fifty yards further along.'

★ ★ ★

Rhona took a gulp of hot coffee, but it did little to bring warmth back to her chilled bones. She'd insisted on going back down the sewer with Dr Mackenzie for the *in situ* examination. For once MacKenzie hadn't argued. Maybe being the one to find a body had its compensations.

She then spent half an hour with MacRae viewing the surveillance tapes of Princes Street on the night of the fire. Three men were caught on camera passing the building.

'The one on the left could be our decomposing body,' MacRae suggested.

'Maybe. But it would need computer enhancement to prove it. What about the other two?'

'Never seen them before in my life. They're there, then they disappear,' MacRae said. 'But that doesn't mean they went into the building. They might just have turned up into George Street.'

'We can check a DNA sample from the sewer body against the semen in Karen's body.'

'He's dead, she's dead,' MacRae said. 'What's the point?'

'Then we'll check it against the letter.'

MacRae shrugged. They were no nearer the fire-raiser now than they'd ever been. They'd found a body in a sewer. Even if he was the rapist, it didn't mean he had anything to do with the fire. Whoever had run from them in the sewer might have.

MacRae fished in his pocket and handed her an envelope. 'MacFarlane asked me to give you this.'

Rhona tore it open. She read the faxed forensic report on the remaining cups with growing alarm.

MacRae hadn't trusted Jaz from the outset. Did Jaz give them the drawing already knowing the guy was dead? Jaz had been watching Greg's apartment and MacRae's family. Jaz drank coffee in Greg's flat. Now they had matched a DNA trace on the semen in the letter with the cup taken from Greg's. Which must mean Jaz sent the letter.'

She grabbed MacRae's arm.

'What the hell's wrong?'

'We have to get inside Greg's apartment.'

31

GREG'S FRONT DOOR swung open.

It had taken just ten seconds for MacRae to defeat the fancy security system.

'You've done this before?'

'Don't tell MacFarlane.'

The flat was clean and empty. There were fresh flowers in a vase on the hall table and a neat pile of unopened mail by the phone.

The bedroom wardrobe revealed a partially cleared rail and no shoes. Rhona was convinced Greg hadn't been there since she spoke to him that first night.

'What are we looking for?'

Rhona was skimming through the telephone book. She found the number and dialled. A man's voice answered.

She tried to sound casual. 'Is Greg there?'

'No,' the voice sounded amused. 'Should he be?' Whoever Justin was he'd changed his voice since their last meeting.

'I believe we met in Greg's flat a few days ago,' Rhona tried. 'You arrived just as I was leaving.'

The voice was puzzled but anxious to help. During the ensuing conversation Rhona learned that Justin

Roberts was not the man who let himself into Greg's flat and sat calmly on the sofa.

By the time she hung up, MacRae had rediscovered the drinks cabinet and was helping himself.

'I need a drink,' he said as if she might argue. He sat down where the pseudo Justin Roberts had sat, feet up, giving her the once-over. That was what had been odd, Rhona realised. She had never been sized up by a gay man before.

'So your friend's gone to Rome. What's the problem?'

A niggling doubt was turning into a terrible realisation.

'I've been stupid.'

'What the hell are you talking about?'

'I gave him a name and an identity.'

MacRae looked lost.

'The second time I stayed . . . there was a guy came into the flat. I assumed it was Greg's boyfriend Justin Roberts.'

MacRae was catching on, fast.

'And it wasn't?'

She shook her head. Everything was adding up. 'I think he's the man we're looking for.'

The drill of the phone interrupted her explanation. The ansaphone cut in and started its bland message. Then a voice Rhona recognised ordered her to pick up.

'Yes?'

There was a short silence, then:

'I want you to know I can see you both quite clearly.'

Rhona looked round, mentally stripping the room, searching for the camera.

'Don't bother. You won't find it.'

'Bast . . .'

Rhona covered MacRae's expletive with her hand. She spoke quietly into the receiver.

'What do you want?'

'We're going to play a little game, you and I. If you win, MacRae's child will live. If you lose, both the building you are in and the granny's cottage will be destroyed by fire.'

Rhona forced her voice to remain calm. The arsonist was power-assertive. Confronting him would only make matters worse. Beside her MacRae's breath was coming in gasps, his skin grey.

'Tell me what to do.'

She listened to his orders, sick at the thought of the consequences of his action. An explosion here would seriously undermine the building, break gas pipes. The arsonist would get his show alright. Bigger and louder than any pyrotechnic display in Princes Street Gardens.

'We have to clear the building first,' she insisted.

'No! he said harshly. 'You have exactly twenty minutes. You will go alone. MacRae will remain in my line of sight. Is that understood?'

'Yes.'

Rhona touched MacRae's arm. 'There's still time. Try and call MacFarlane,' she whispered.

The basement was empty apart from some packing cases lining the walls. But if she had been sent to look, there had to be something to find. It just wouldn't be obvious.

Rhona walked up and down, stamping to check the sound. Nothing. She headed diagonally towards the opposite wall. This time the sound was different. She was a foot from the corner. Four packing cases stood between her and the wall. She dragged them back.

A narrow set of steps led to a darkened room below street level. At the bottom a sewer vent pipe climbed the wall.

MacRae's voice echoed in her head. 'Every building has a six-inch-diameter pipe leading into the sewer. They don't all have a way in.'

Rhona wouldn't believe that. Couldn't.

She dropped to her knees on the rough concrete floor and began to crawl about, exploring the surface with her hands.

The metal ring of the manhole cover jabbed her shin. She grabbed it and pulled, in a paroxysm of effort. Sewer gas escaped from the black hole, making her gag. She braced herself and dropped inside.

Propane was denser than air. If the gas was already on it would have gathered below. He would set the timer to spark ignition ten minutes later.

She stood trying to get her bearings. Running alongside, the muted flow of water was barely audible. As her eyes became accustomed to the dark, she made out a door on her left and reached for the handle.

Inside was a pair of overalls, an assortment of tools and a torch. As she switched on the torch, she caught the scent of gas.

Now was the time to run. Her heart was racing. How long did she have? If he had been lying to her, then death was imminent. If he was telling the truth, she had five minutes to find the propane and stop it igniting.

In her head time rushed past, yet in the claustrophobic atmosphere of the tunnel it stood still. Breathing as shallowly as possible, she followed the sickening hiss of the gas.

The canisters stood side by side, hidden behind an archway that led from one sewer into the next. Attached was the trigger device. Simple and effective. A spark in a gas-filled area. A memory of the carnage of an IRA terrorist bomb in the height of the Troubles flooded Rhona's head. Forensic bags full of samples that had occupied her days and filled her nights with tortured images of the dead. This explosion would wreak the same havoc.

As in the moments before death she thought of those she cared about. Liam, Sean . . . Severino waiting above, his child in the hands of a madman.

She pulled off her jacket, immersed it in the dark water then walked towards the device.

Sev stood in the same moment of time. In his mind his arms were about Amy, sheltering her from the fire that would rage round her. The scars on his back burned with the memory of his own pain and the pain that would be hers. He wept silently for what he had done to his daughter. He found himself praying. God, let there be angels. God, let Amy's guardian angel protect her. Please God, protect Rhona.

He had turned on the mobile in his pocket and

pressed what he thought was the key for MacFarlane. He'd whispered his message and hoped it was heard.

All his fears about this arsonist had come true. He had focused on the woman, given her a task that could not be fulfilled. He would gloat over her failure. Rhona's death in that fire, his own death, Amy's death, reduced to a snuff movie.

Severino could feel the eyes of the camera on him. Taste the watcher's excitement. He understood it. He had tasted it himself. Fire. The ultimate cleanser. The ultimate life force. The ultimate orgasm.

She forced the small black box under the water, jamming it below the side ledge. Air bubbled to the surface and dissipated. She got off her knees and walked back to the canisters, turning the valves until the hissing stopped.

She stumbled towards the steps, waves of nausea sweeping over her. Her body moved into shock, her limbs shaking with fear, relief and cold.

Sirens announced the imminent arrival of fire engines. She heard voices from the basement; MacFarlane's, then MacRae's, both edged with fear.

'Rhona! Thank Christ!'

Severino caught her as she stumbled up the steps and gathered her in his arms.

She looked up at him.

'Amy?' she said.

32

ABOVE HIM THE skylight was shrouded in white cloud. Jaz reached over and flicked on the bedside lamp. This time he had been asleep. Well and truly asleep.

The room was chilly, the radiator cold. He reached for his jacket. He would check on Emps. Make sure he was alright.

Outside, a single line of footprints led to the cottage. Someone had arrived here recently. But who?

Jaz crept forward, conscious of the crunch of his feet in the snow. The front door was off the latch. He slipped into the hall and stood listening.

Someone was weeping, a small pitiful sound like a child. Amy?

He pushed open the kitchen door. Amy sat in the chair beside the Aga, a teddy bear clasped in her arms, her face streaked with tears.

'Amy. What's wrong?' His eyes darted to the empty dog basket. 'Where's Emps?'

Tommy stepped into view. 'Thought I told you to get lost.'

Jaz looked at Amy's terrified face. 'Amy, come here.'

Amy tried to get up, but Tommy caught her arm and wrenched her back, holding the knife to her neck.

'Amy's not going anywhere, Jazzy-boy, and neither are you.'

Jaz stood still. The most important thing was to get Tommy away from Amy. If he could get him outside, confuse him in the dark, she might have a chance.

Jaz sprang through the open door, ran the length of the hall and dived into the open air, slamming the door behind him. Tommy was seconds after, promising to slit Jaz's fucking throat from ear to ear.

The hedge round the house was at least three feet thick. He could hide in there and wait until Tommy came by.

Tommy was outside now, sweeping the beam of a torch across the front garden. On the third swing, the beam hovered above Jaz then descended, exposing his hiding place and blinding his eyes.

Tommy laughed, a horrible sound. But he was so intent on mocking his prey he hadn't spotted Emperor crawling belly-down towards him across the snow.

As the dog cannoned into Tommy, knocking him to the ground, Amy came running out of the cottage. Jaz grabbed her and made a dash for the front door, meeting the edge of Tommy's knife on the way.

Emps started barking as lights sprang from the trees and half a dozen armed policemen came running across the snow towards the cottage.

33

RHONA WALKED ROUND the lab, touching the equipment which structured her life.

She had stopped the arsonist blowing up the Edinburgh building. Amy was safe. Safe and sound and as far away from her father as Gillian could manage. But they hadn't found the pyromaniac . . . yet.

Outside, January light touched the dripping skeleton branches of trees. Kelvingrove Park had survived the New Year celebrations. As had she. A new year had begun, for Glasgow and for her. Sean had returned. Unexpected and – she toyed with the idea – almost unwelcome.

Fear of death was erotic. She and Severino had tasted that fear together. It was worth everything in that moment . . . but when fear subsided?

Her mobile drilled a sharp note. She glanced at the screen, expecting Sean's name.

It was Liam.

She pressed the green key and waited, holding her breath.

His voice sounded improbably young. She conjured a vision of him in her head, as she had done a thousand times before.

'Can I come and see you?'

'I'd like that.'

He stumbled. 'I'm sorry . . .'

She stopped him. 'It doesn't matter.'

'I was scared.'

Relief swept over her. So that was why he hadn't turned up.

'So was I.'

There was a silence.

'I'll be there in half an hour,' he said.

She whispered 'Okay' and hung up.

She concentrated on the details of the case while she waited for Liam to arrive.

The body in the sewer was the guy in Jaz's drawing. His name was Joe MacMurdo. He was known to the Glasgow force as a small-time drug dealer. MacMurdo's DNA had matched the semen found in Karen. It looked like Karen had been raped by MacMurdo then left to die in the fire. After all, who cares about a homeless girl without a family? But Jaz had cared enough to put his own life in danger, she reminded herself.

Soon all the pieces would come together. The process had already begun. DI Wilson had passed details of Meldrum Holdings to the Procurator Fiscal. With Jaz's statement on what he had overheard between Tommy and the Financial Director of Meldrum Holdings, they thought they had a case of intimidation and murder associated with the company. Bill Wilson suspected the Finance Director for Meldrum Holdings would be the fall guy. Already the big guns behind the company were marshalling their lawyers, pleading ignorance of any crooked dealing.

Tommy Moffat was in the frame for MacMurdo's murder and being involved in the rape. If Tommy thought they had enough on him, he might squeal about Meldrum Holdings in the hope of a reduced sentence.

They had already established that he had been cutting the drugs with anything he could find, including the white stuff his wee brother brought home from the fireworks factory. Tommy had it both ways: he made money from dealing, then picked up his hit money as the addicts died off and left the schemes empty for Meldrum Holdings to develop.

The arsonist was the enigma. Severino had tried to persuade her to have a police guard until they picked him up, but that seemed too melodramatic for Rhona. Security was tight in the lab already. Having a policeman stand around all day getting bored was overkill.

She glanced at the clock. Where was Chrissy? She'd only gone to drop off a forensic bag at Chemistry. She should have been back by now.

She checked the window. Liam should be arriving any moment. Sure enough, a tall, blond figure was coming across the car park. She watched the long-legged stride. Saw him hesitate then approach the gate guard. They both looked up at her window. Rhona stepped back, her heart hammering, her mouth dry.

She was terrified to meet her own child. Frightened of what she would see in his eyes.

The lab phone rang. She didn't move. If she met Liam, things would never be the same again, for either of them. Sweat broke out on her brow as the phone continued to ring. She steeled herself and picked up.

'Dr MacLeod?'

'Yes?'

'I have a young man in reception called Liam Hope. Says he's here to see you.'

She asked the security guard to send him up, her voice sounding like someone else. She should have gone down to meet him, but she couldn't trust her legs to carry her.

She was facing the door, waiting for Liam's silhouette to appear in the small pane of glass. The movement behind her caused her to turn, thinking Chrissy had returned unnoticed.

Severino stood behind her, dressed in a white lab coat, a visitor badge pinned to his lapel. He smiled. She opened her mouth to ask how he had got in, then realised it wasn't Sev, merely a caricature of him.

The man from Greg's apartment wasn't smiling this time, and he wasn't embarrassed. The blond hair had been dyed black, the glasses discarded.

'How the hell . . . ?

She didn't get to finish. He caught her arm and twisted it up her back. The pain was excruciating.

She thrust her free hand backwards, hoping to hit him in the crotch. He laughed, pushing her elbow even higher. Her mouth filled with bile as nausea swept over her.

'Do that again and I'll break your arm.'

She responded through clenched teeth, thinking all the time of Liam's imminent arrival.

'What do you want?'

He stiffened, hearing the footsteps in the corridor.

'Please God, no,' she whispered.

Then she heard the knock at the door and saw the tall silhouette behind the glass.

'Who is it?' he spat in her ear.

'I don't know,' she lied.

'Tell them you're busy.'

The knock came again.

'Sorry, I'm busy.' Her voice sounded cold and remote. 'Can you come back later?'

Rhona willed Liam to walk away, but he wasn't giving up this time.

There was a moment's silence then, 'Rhona?' He pressed his face against the glass. 'Please. It's me, Liam.'

The door began to open.

A rush of fear and love swamped Rhona.

'No!' she cried as the cold metal of a gun met her ribs.

Her son's face was startled.

Liam looked down at the gun then up at her face.

'Get inside, now!'

Liam did as he was told.

'Shut the door and lock it.' The man looked Liam up and down. 'Who are you?'

'Dr MacLeod's son.'

There was a moment's silence.

'Now that's one thing I didn't know about Dr MacLeod.'

Even the cynical voice reminded her of Sev.

Rhona edged her body between the gun and Liam. Chrissy would appear any minute. She just had to stay calm and keep him talking.

'Why are you here?' she tried.

'I made you a promise. I came to keep it.'

'What's he talking about?' Liam asked.

Rhona threw Liam a look, willing him to stay calm.

'You're very like MacRae,' she suggested.

A flash of anger crossed his face.

'That bastard ruined my life.'

'How did he do that?'

'They threw me out of the Brigade because of him.'

He waved them towards the sample cupboard at the back of the lab and pushed them inside.

Rhona grabbed Liam's hand, squeezing it tightly. His pulse beat swiftly in the nape of his neck, but his face was resolved. He wasn't going to panic. Yet.

The door snapped shut behind them and the key turned.

'What did he mean, what he promised?'

The mix of letters in those emails rearranged themselves in Rhona's head.

BURN THE BITCH. That was his promise.

'Security will be here soon,' she told Liam, wishing she believed it herself.

A new sprinkler system had been installed the previous year. If it worked they had a chance, provided the smoke didn't get them first.

She heard him moving about the lab, piling stuff

against the cupboard door. Then the crackle as the paper caught.

Smoke began to drift under the door.

'The sprinklers will come on,' she told Liam.

But they didn't.

The smoke was thickening. Where the hell was the alarm and the sprinklers? Liam's face was grey with fear. She pulled off her lab coat and thrust it at him.

'Cover your mouth with this.'

At the back was a panel that led to the riser, a shaft that ran up through the building. It housed the network and power cables and more recently the sprinkler pipes when they did up the lab. It also had a metal ladder. But the panel needed a maintenance key to open it. Liam was watching her, his eyes bloodshot and streaming above the lab coat. She looked wildly about her for something to force the lock.

'Here. Try this.'

He thrust a Swiss army knife into her hand. He had flicked open a blade and she inserted it into the lock. It really needed a round key, but it might work. She was praying out loud as she felt the blade turn. There was a resistance then a sudden click. Tears streamed down her face as the panel dropped forward.

Air rushed down the shaft, escaping through into the lab, feeding the fire even more.

'Can you climb?'

Liam looked up.

'I think so.'

'There's an opening into the room above. Look for a

panel on the left of the shaft. You'll have to force it open.'

'What about you?'

'I'll follow,' she promised.

She watched his feet disappear. What the hell had happened to the smoke alarms and all the fancy computer-controlled equipment they'd installed last year?

She had brought Liam here. If her son died it would be her fault.

She began to climb.

Liam had reached the panel. The shaft was full of smoke and she couldn't see him, but she could hear him battering the wall.

It was too late. The fumes had seeped into every part of her. Her brain, her stomach, her lungs. She couldn't fight for breath any more.

Then she heard the alarm go off, a glorious shrieking sound, as smoke escaped with Liam into the next level.

Liam was out. That was all she cared about.

She closed her eyes and let go.

'Rhona!'

Liam's voice was a thousand miles away, but his hand held hers and he was pulling her free.

34

JAZ STUDIED THE headstone.

In Memory of
Karen Carlyle
18th August 1989–28th December 2004
Aged 15 yrs
Love
Jaz and Emperor

At least there had been someone at her funeral. Rhona came. But not Liam. He had left to work in Africa for a year. She pretended she was alright about that, but Jaz knew by her eyes that she wasn't. DI MacFarlane was there, and DI Wilson.

And MacRae, looking like shit. Glancing all the time at Rhona as if he wanted to say something, and couldn't. MacRae had told him Amy had wanted to come but her mother wouldn't let her. Jaz didn't blame the mother for that. A funeral wasn't the place for a wee girl.

It had taken a while to find out who Karen was, but MacFarlane promised he would do it, and he had.

Emps put his cold nose in Jaz's hand.

'Okay, boy. Let's go.'

He set off across the frosted grass, Emps running by his side. Karen's death had made him even more determined not to screw up this time. He owed it to her. He had started evening classes at college, was painting again. He planned to paint Karen the way he remembered her. In Rose Street, playing the penny whistle. That way, she would always be alive.

'I didn't sleep with him.'

Sean's eyes held hers. 'It doesn't matter.'

'Then what does?' she said sharply.

He ran his fingers through his hair. He didn't want to argue when the outcome was inevitable. He took her hand and stroked the palm with his thumb.

'I'm not asking you to go,' she said defensively.

He lifted her hand and kissed it, sending a shiver through her body.

'You met someone in Amsterdam.' If that were true, it would make it easier.

He shook his head. 'This isn't about me.'

'You need space to decide . . .' The words *who you want* were left unsaid. 'I'll be in my old room at the club . . . if you need me.'

He let her hand fall. It felt cold without him.

'You'll come and hear me on Friday?'

She nodded. She wanted to kiss him, but didn't.

She'd felt frightened as he left. Frightened to be alone. It lasted until the door closed behind him. Then she felt relief.

She stood in the empty flat. Sean's suitcase gone from the hall, the saxophone from the corner of the bedroom.

So that was it.

She tested her feelings, recognising the hole that Sean's departure had left inside her.

She had told him Sev had stayed at the flat on Hogmanay and held her in his arms as the bells tolled in the New Year, because in those moments they both needed someone. That was all, she'd insisted, and almost meant it. Sean had read between the lines.

The cat came and wrapped itself round her legs in a flurry of cupboard love.

'Just you and me again.'

She picked Chance up and carried him into the kitchen. The grass in the convent garden below the window was frosted icing. Two nuns were strolling around, their footprints criss-crossing the white topping. If only her world was like theirs: calm, peaceful and orderly.

Since the fire in the laboratory, she had lost all the men in her life. Liam had promised to write, but he was going somewhere remote. A school on the Nigeria-Cameroon border. She wouldn't hear from him very often. She wondered if she ever would.

That last night they'd sat in a bar in Byres Road, where the surrounding noise made conversation easier. He was interested in her work and worried for her safety. She found herself liking this young man she had loved from a distance for so long.

Watching his face as he spoke, she thought she

detected both herself and Edward in him. She didn't regret either resemblance, because Liam was his own man. She asked if he would like to know who his father was.

'Not if you don't want to tell me.'

She told him everything. How much she had loved Edward, how wrong she had been to give her son up. 'I've thought about you every day of my life.' She looked down, not wanting him to see the tears in her eyes.

He was silent for a moment, giving her time.

'I had a happy childhood. But there were things about me I didn't understand . . .' He paused, trying to put his thoughts into words. 'I liked being alone.' He gave a half smile. 'Mum and Dad thought I was lonely.'

'And were you?'

He shook his head. 'No. But when they told me about the adoption, I understood why I was different.'

They had begun to talk of other things. His trip to Africa, his university course, her work.

She suspected that, like her, he needed to go away and think about this. He had met her once. Maybe that was all he needed or wanted. When they parted he turned and waved, and she took a mental image of her son to hold close to her in case she never saw him again.

Severino too had come to see her, blaming himself for her ordeal. She'd had a hunch about the arsonist and he didn't act on it quickly enough.

Tim Redpath had served with the fire service for ten

years. He had been dedicated to the work. Some said, consumed by it. Fire became more important than anything else in his life. Like me, Severino said. He was suspected of starting some of the fires he attended and had been dismissed from the service. His life fell apart. When he started buying drugs, Tommy Moffat had seen the potential in Tim's obsession.

'And the connection with Greg?'

'Once he established where you were staying, he did a bit of detective work,' he paused. 'If I had been thinking more and drinking less . . .' Sev's voice tailed off. 'I'm sorry.'

'For what?'

He looked at the suitcase waiting in the hall.

'For fucking up your life.'

'I managed that all by myself.'

He met her eyes.

'Do you think, you and I . . .'

She ran it over in her head, not for the first time.

'No.'

'I had to ask.'

When they kissed, his breath was sweet.

'Irn-Bru.' He smiled wryly.

She drew away.

'What about Gillian?'

'Moving to Auchenblair permanently. There's a nice steady guy there. Runs the local hotel. He's always had a soft spot for Gillian. Amy's going to the village school.'

'I'm sorry.'

'You're not the only one who can mess up.' He stroked her face. 'What will you do now?'

'Go back to work.'

'We're alike, you and I.'

'That would be the problem.'

Rhona listened to the silence, then walked from room to room reclaiming her home. Sean was right. She needed time and space. If they got back together it would be on different terms. They would each have to learn to commit.

She felt a strange peace envelop her. She had found Liam. The arsonist was caught. And she knew at last that her nemesis was dead. The forensic tests on the remains found in the hills were complete. Weakened by loss of blood, he had died of exposure. The paedophile who called himself Simon would never again trawl the internet for vulnerable young men. She need never search for him in a crowd again.

The convent bells began to toll for evening prayer. Rhona carried the cat into the sitting-room, switched on the stereo and sat down in front of the fire as the saxophone's notes filled the air.

Alone, Rhona listened to it play its song of love.